W0007820

To Prince Edward Island—thank you for
the inspiration.

Chapter One

RUBY ZALONSKI GLANCED out the wide windows at the rain-soaked Simmons College campus lawn. The black umbrellas most students carried intermingled with the occasional pink polka-dot or sunny yellow one, in the heart of downtown Boston's Fenway neighborhood.

Gray clouds scuttled across the August sky. The fat raindrops plopped against the windowpanes of LeFavour Hall, which housed the library at Simmons College.

Ruby sat in an overstuffed chair in the archives room of the library. She took a deep breath and inhaled the cozy and familiar scent of musty paper and waxed hardwood floors. A smile flitted across her face as her eyelids fluttered closed.

For a second, she imagined herself ten years in the future: a nice tenure-track archival position here at Simmons in the library and information science department, living in a historic brownstone, and married to a nice man. She sighed. Then maybe she'd finally feel like she belonged here? Had a real *home*?

She fiddled with the antique heart-shaped locket she wore around her neck.

Never mind that she'd lived in Boston all her life. So it *was* her real home. She let the sterling silver necklace slide through her fingers. But this place, this city, just didn't feel like that.

She didn't quite know why. But she'd always had this vague sense of restlessness. As if she belonged somewhere else. Should *be* somewhere else.

She tapped an unpolished fingernail against her chin as she looked down at the antique love letter fragment. Its edges were torn and what looked like smudges of dirt and gunpowder obscured the neat, curving script.

Though the iron gall ink had faded to a reddish brown, the flourishes of the t's, dots of the i's and flowing lines of the f's remained strong. Defiant.

She broke into a grin.

Even...revolutionary.

Boston 2 Dec. 1775

My darling Edwina.

In the fortnight since I was taken from you, I can but think only of the August night we met, when such horrors of war were furthest from our minds, and I daresay, our hearts, as well.

Though I must confess, I did not think of you as attentive to my affections when I was greeted by dawn gleaming off the blade of your cutlass that November morn. How the compass of the heart points in new directions when time and distance have no little significance.

News in Charlotte Town travels at speed, especially among those who frequent Cross Keys Tavern, myself among them. I know you can imagine my state of appal when I, one week prior, learned of your Situation. That General Washington and his Rebellious Colonies should treat Callbeck and Wright with such deference and kindness, but leave you to your fate in the hands of those Loyal to the Crown, I do not conceive.

I fear that I may never again see your sweet face—

Ruby sighed. It was too bad Dr. O'Neil hadn't had the other half of the letter fragment like she'd hoped he would. But this couldn't be a dead end. It just couldn't. Her dissertation was riding on Revolutionary War love letters like this one.

Where was the other half of this letter? What did the rest of it say? And, most of all, *who* was writing to Edwina?

Ruby's eyes traced the jagged, ripped edge. Her contact at the rare books store on Cambridge Avenue found this fragment in an old family bible they'd had on display.

Just then, the library clock tower gonged the hour. She scrambled to her feet. How had it gotten to be 5 p.m. already?

She had to hurry or she'd be late for that first date tonight.

After she gathered the rest of the notes she needed, Ruby made her way out of the library and back across the green expanse of lawn to the library sciences department.

She wove her way through the maze of graduate and doctoral students, dropped backpacks and makeshift desks before she finally reached her own desk, shoved into a tiny alcove under the eaves, to transcribe what she'd found.

She lifted the lid of her old, somewhat glitchy silver Macbook. Its edges bristled with bright pink, blue and yellow sticky notes to herself. The ding of an incoming email made her pause.

To. ruby.zalonski@simmons.edu
Sent: Monday, August 12

A note to all current staff and students. The position of special collections & archival librarian, payband 12, has been posted as of this email, with the retirement of longtime employee Marianne Schwartz, who has been with us for 30 years.

There will be a retirement party on Tuesday afternoon for her. So don't forget to stop by the staff lounge for some cake and coffee, and a chance to find out what Marianne will be doing with her retirement!

The position was finally opening up? A little thrill ran through Ruby. She opened up a new outgoing message and attached her resume and cover letter, then hit send. She grinned.

Now, she had to finish transcribing her notes.

She readjusted the No. 2 pencil that secured her messy brunette bun and pushed her cat-eye tortoiseshell glasses further up on her nose. Her fingers stilled on the keyboard as her mind strayed back to the letter fragment.

The bold, sweeping handwriting formed in her mind's eye. No one wrote like that these days.

The way the quill pen had formed each word with a hint of a flourish.

She found herself holding her breath as she recalled the writer's firm belief in Edwina's love. The tender words...

For a second she wished whoever it was had been addressing her. Because she'd never find a love that grand. That sweeping. That, well, legendary...

"Ruby? How's it going?"

She glanced over her shoulder. Dr. Jill Burton, the department head—and Ruby's academic advisor for her doctoral dissertation *In Love & War: A Discourse on Women's Love Letters During The American Revolution*—leaned into the half-open doorway. Dr. Burton crossed one lime-green ballet flat over the other.

"Pretty good, Dr. Burton. Did you know that the special collections position just opened up?" Ruby shuffled the pages of notes on her desk before looking back up at the older woman.

Dr. Burton nodded. "Saw that a minute ago—was about to tell you."

"I just applied." Ruby blurted. "I know I haven't completed my Ph.D. yet. But if I could be considered for that job, it would be a dream come true." She grinned.

The older woman smiled. "While I'm all in favor of your enthusiasm, you do know that a Ph.D. is one of the requirements? They do consider non-Ph.D.'s at a university of this size. But it's rare that someone without a Ph.D.—even someone like you who's almost completed her doctorate—would be chosen. Besides that, competition will be fierce. There hasn't been an opening like this in 30 years."

"I know." Ruby said, and pushed up her glasses.

Dr. Burton smiled again. "Well, if I hear anything about when they want to start interviewing, I'll definitely keep you in the loop. So how's everything coming? Your dissertation is in committee review right now. Which means your defense date is coming up pretty fast. Early next month."

"If I could find more of Edwina's letters, it would definitely support my main theory about women's love letters in the

American Revolution as a vital means of communication and self-expression." She paused. "I'm not prone to conspiracy theories, but whoever was writing to her, I think there was something going on...I know that it doesn't exactly have a direct connection to my original love letter research, but it might be an interesting side note or sub-theory to work in."

"Just make sure there's enough money left in your research grant to go ahead with it. They won't be giving out more funds any time soon." Dr. Burton cocked her head. She tapped a French-tipped fingernail against her chin, a sparkle in her eye. "But you're right—that sounds pretty interesting. It certainly wouldn't hurt to explore that angle. It might even add new evidence you could work into your defense. Make it stand apart."

Ruby laughed. "Thanks! So, what's the latest on those papers of Dr. O'Neil's?"

"It's too bad about his passing away so suddenly." Dr. Burton shook her head. "I just got back from a meeting about the late professor." The older woman crossed her arms, and a frown formed between her perfectly plucked brows. "I don't know how it happened in this economic climate—especially with so much money being re-directed to the sports program."

"But," Dr. Burton continued, "the university lawyers have all been consulted, and the paperwork's all drawn up, so it's been given the go-ahead. Which means our department will finally be able to receive his donated papers. Now we just need someone to go up and catalog them."

Wait a minute. A smile spread across Ruby's lips. Special collections…"You need someone to catalog Dr. O'Neil's papers— why not me?" Ruby's heart thudded. "After all, I initiated contact with Dr. O'Neil in the first place—eight months ago—asking him about that love letter fragment to Edwina."

If she cataloged his papers, then it'd be apparent to all of them here on campus that she was the ideal candidate for that special collections position, Ph.D. or no Ph.D.

"He had so many historical documents," Ruby added. "If I went up there, maybe I could find other love letters written by and to, Edwina, that would help my overall research and add to my supporting documents."

And it would be the perfect opportunity to distinguish herself from the other candidates. She could prove she'd gone above and beyond. Acquired and cataloged this special cache of documents. It'd be easy enough to organize the professor's papers, surely.

"Well, Ruby, you have a good point. All right, the cataloging job's yours. But just remember, you need to be back here by next Thursday so you can prep for your doctoral defense."

"Right," Ruby said. "I'm sure the cataloging won't take long."

THE SALTY AIR riffled the sparkling blue water of Charlottetown Harbor and buffeted against the forest green of Nathan O'Neil's jacket. He stood on the grassy slope of the earthworks of Fort Amherst, at the Skmaqn-Port-la-Joye-Fort Amherst National Historic Site, which nestled against the red cliffs of Prince Edward Island.

He took a deep breath. Couldn't imagine living anywhere else than here on the island. It was home.

This view was one he'd always loved. Bathed in August afternoon light, the boats trailed wakes through the waves. The Charlottetown cityscape was just barely visible from across the bay.

In fact...this would make a great drawing. On impulse, he pulled out the tiny spiral-bound notebook and pencil he always kept in his jeans pocket.

Hmm, the cliffs would look better if he moved more to the left. He applied pencil to paper and sketched the sparkling waterfront scene. He paused. Looked up again. Cocked his head. If this sketch was going to work, he'd need to add just a bit more detail to the waves...

He glanced at his watch. How had twenty minutes gone by? His coffee break was definitely up. Well, that server issue wasn't going to fix itself. He needed to get back and reboot everything.

He strode up the grassy slope. Then headed onto the gravel path that wound its way through a pine grove leading up to the site's interpretive center. The scent of wild roses drifted to him. He glanced at the row of bushes that bordered the pathway. The plaque near them stated they were descended from original plantings done in the 1700s.

"Hi, how are ya, Nathan?" the man behind the counter said, "Before you go over to the servers, can you check in the back room?"

"Rick, we've known each other since

we were eight. You know I'm not exactly a handyman."

Both men chuckled.

"The men's room ran out of paper towel with that last tour bus load. There's another set to show up any minute. The janitor doesn't come on shift for two more hours, and I'm swamped answering calls and giving tours. Otherwise I'd run in there and do it myself."

"All right, I'll go do it. But only because you saved me from getting a swirly from Bobby McPhee back in grade five."

Nathan unlocked the storeroom and rummaged through the cardboard boxes until he found a box full of brown paper towelling. He re-locked the storeroom and headed toward the men's room.

His head brushed the brick ceiling as he stepped inside the washroom. Going into this place always unnerved him. He glanced around the cramped space. Its walls, ceiling and floors seemed to slough off more crumbling brick every day.

God, how old was this place? He didn't know.

But he did know it was always damp. And that this section, converted in the 1960s before they'd been so vigilant about conservation, used to be part of the old jail, back when Fort Amherst was in use.

He rubbed his arms against the chill that had crept under his forest green fleece jacket. Then again, he was pretty much always cold.

He shifted the box of paper towelling to the rough, uneven floor, and leaned over it to get to the paper towel dispenser.

He jiggled the lock, but it wouldn't budge. Even with the key.

With a muttered curse, he nudged the paper towel box aside so he could stand as close as possible to the dispenser.

He slid the key into the tiny lock again and twisted. Still nothing. He shook the dispenser gently and hoped it would jar something loose.

Still nothing.

Maybe there was another way to open it? Nathan inspected it from all angles. He finally spotted a narrow gap along the bottom, one that would just fit his fingertips. Worth a shot. He slid his fingers into the slight space and pried upward.

Nothing.

He tugged a little harder. With a bang, the dispenser front flopped open, hit the brick wall and caused Nathan to jump backward. He lost his balance, and held onto the only thing that kept him upright:

the towel dispenser.

But it pulled away from the wall with a grating and scraping noise. Nathan fell backwards. He landed on the rough brick floor.

He winced. Caught his breath. Hmmm, nothing...broken.

He got up. Dusted himself off and put the new paper towel roll into the holder then glanced down at the box on the floor.

He glanced back up at the wall. And swore.

There was a gaping hole in the wall.

He leaned forward to inspect it. He brushed aside the crumbling mortar and brick dust as his fingers explored the empty cavity. Well, he'd have to—

His fingers brushed something soft. Cloth, he realized. Tucked in behind the left edge of the cavity.

He tugged on it, and it ripped. He swore again.

He tugged on it more gingerly this time and finally pulled it free. It was a tiny, lightweight bundle, wrapped in some sort of yellowed fabric.

He coughed at the swirl of dust as he unfolded the cloth.

It was...a book?

No, he realized, not a book: a notebook

---

of sorts. A journal? He eased open the cover. No name there.

Hmmm.

He opened the first page.

But there was nothing written on it. He flipped to the middle. Nothing there either. The book's pages were completely blank. Every last one. Hmmm.

Just then, the door swung open and an Asian man stuck his head into the room.

On an impulse Nathan couldn't explain, he shoved the small book into the inside pocket of his jacket. "I'll let you just—uh, there you go." Nathan gestured to the paper towel and ducked out of the washroom.

After he brushed the mortar and dust off his jacket, Nathan headed back to the desk. "I think the maintenance guy will have to be called in a bit sooner than his usual shift. That paper towel dispenser needs looking at."

THE LIBRARY CLOCK tower gonged a final time and Ruby looked up from the computer screen. It was 6 p.m. She really had to get going. But before she shut down her laptop, she glanced once more at the final email Dr. O'Neil had sent her.

From: goneil@upei.ca
To: ruby.zalonski@simmons.edu
Subject: 1775 letter fragment
Sent: January 12

Dear Ruby,

Thank you for your email last week. I apologize for the delay in responding to you. There have been a few issues that have come up, but I'm sure they will blow over. I've weathered such storms before. The dean and some of my colleagues don't seem to like the theories I'm formulating about Edwina Belliveaux. (Another reason I'm planning to donate my papers to your department at Simmons instead of here at UPEI, once I finally decide to retire for good.)

Anyway, after studying the letter fragment scan you enclosed, I'm sorry to say that I don't have the other half. Though women's love letters during the American Revolution certainly makes for intriguing research.

Because we're both researching Edwina—though for very different reasons—I did some digging in my personal papers since we last corre-sponded.

And came across General Wash-ington's signed order of Nov. 23, which mentions Edwina. I thought it might be of interest for your own work, so I've attached a copy to this message.

This order is the last remaining original copy. You know, it was only by chance I came across it, pressed between the pages of a psalm book I'd gotten at a rare book auction near Boston some years ago. I've been working on my theory ever since.

You mentioned you don't know the story behind Edwina's role in trying to prevent the theft of the Great Seal of Prince Edward Island, so allow me to fill you in. My version is a bit more complete than the Wik-ipedia entry.

Near dawn on November 17, 1775, a group of American priva-teers, helmed by Captain John Selman and Captain Nicholas Broughton, both under the command of General George Washington, diso-beyed a direct order from Washing-ton (which I've also attached), and set sail for Charlottetown, Prince Edward Island. (But back then it was called St. John's Island.) They were supposed to lay in wait for British ships carrying arms and supplies to Quebec, along the St. Lawrence River, but for reasons lost to history, decided to head to P.E.I. instead.

Two American tall ships were in the harbour that morning. Governor Walter Patterson was away in England. So the acting governor, Phillips Callbeck, went down to the docks, hoping to talk some sense into the Americans. Poor man—he'd only been at the post four months. He couldn't stop the Americans. They began raiding and looting the town. Callbeck got kidnapped. Thomas Wright, the town surveyor, who just happened to be in the wrong place at the wrong time, got kidnapped too. Such was the fate of another young man, who got kidnapped as well. But his name, unfortunately, has been lost.

The Americans took all of Charlottetown's winter supplies. They also stole the Great Seal of Prince Edward Island, which was made of silver. But *not before Miss Edwina Belliveaux tried to stop them.*

I don't know about down there, but up here on Prince Edward Island, people see Edwina Belliveaux as a heroic historical figure. She is famously known for saying, "Unhand that seal, good sir. It is not, nor ever shall be, yours."

But they took it anyway.

The privateers sailed back to Massachusetts. Washington demoted the two captains and freed Callbeck and Wright. Nothing is said of what happened to the young man. But the Americans did keep all the winter supplies, as well as the Great Seal. The seal's never been found. Not only that, there's still a reward of £1000 for its safe return.

I believe that the lost seal can be found and that the reward money may be partial proof of this. I'm also inclined to speculate that the seal may be part of something larger— perhaps a treasure of sorts? (My family seems to think I spend a little too much time speculating on this. And my colleagues, well, let's just say they think I'm completely wrong. But I say what's academics if you don't have a little disagreement?)

What's more, after reading the love letter fragment, in conjunction with Washington's Nov. 23 order, I think my theory about Edwina stealing the seal is correct. (For the treasure?) If so, it just may change the history books, and lead me one step closer to finding the lost seal...I'll be in touch soon.

Dr. Gordon O'Neil
Professor Emeritus of P.E.I. History
Department of History
University of Prince Edward Island

Ruby shut her laptop. She stuffed the last papers into her bag and headed outside. She dodged puddles as she hurried across the lush green lawn. Just as she headed off campus and caught a tram headed in the direction of Boston Common, her phone buzzed. She glanced at it and grinned at the name on the caller ID. "Hey, Maggie!"

"Hi, Ruby. How's it going?"

"Oh, good, good. Just running late for a first date."

"This the one with that banker tonight?"

"No, that was last month." Ruby sighed. "I ended that after the third date."

"He hit the third-date cliff, did he?" Maggie teased.

"Yeah...I don't know why I do that. Seems I'm always ending things after the third date. Who knows? I'm probably just afraid of commitment or something." She bit her lip. "I'm afraid that—I know this sounds kind of ridiculous—the guy will just disappear on me. So I guess I feel safer if I end things before he gets a chance to."

"Aww, well, good luck with this one."

"Thanks. How's that new jewelry design coming?"

"That antique locket of yours really got me inspired. Oh! I have to run. Got a meeting with one of my suppliers but just wanted to wish you luck tonight."

AFTER WORK, NATHAN jumped in the shower. Fifteen minutes later, he tucked a blue paisley-print towel firmly around his waist.

He wiped away the steam from the mirror in his bathroom. He flicked on the electric razor then applied shaving cream across his dark stubble and started to use the shaver. Why did he keep breaking things off with perfectly good women? Especially after going so far as to get engaged. Twice.

He shook his head.

He finished shaving and flicked off the razor. Maybe this woman would turn out to be his true love... Where had *that* come from?

Because true love, well, it didn't exist. It was a myth. A legend. Just like that island poem called *The Fair Isle Lovers*. Something beautiful, but something unreal. A figment of the imagination. And most of all: impossible.

Women loved that poem. It was full of passion and romance.

He pursed his lips. And tragedy.

He shook his head. He could never figure out quite why every schoolkid on the island—including himself—had to memorize it in grade six. It had a pretty depressing ending, now that he thought about it...

Kind of like his relationships. Hadn't all his relationships, if you could even call them that, taught him that? Love was always a disappointment. Love was pain. And after the initial high, the initial hope, it all fizzled out.

Fell apart.

When he realized, yet again, that he couldn't drum up the depth of feeling for any of the women. No matter how much he wanted to. No matter how long he stayed.

No matter what, the emptiness persisted. Grew, even. And once he'd broken up with the latest woman, he was inevitably alone. Left picking up the pieces of his disappointment. Yet again.

Just because he'd had two broken engagements didn't mean there was anything wrong with him. Did it?

He ran his fingers through his damp hair but didn't bother with gel. He slapped on some aftershave and then paused. The woodsy scent brought up the usual sense of longing and restlessness he couldn't quite place. Yet he'd bought this bottle because he'd loved the way the aftershave smelled.

A smile flicked across his face. The woodsy scent somehow reminded him of Fort Amherst. He'd always loved it there. Not the fort itself but the woods around it. Well, he shrugged, it was a beautiful spot.

Nathan walked into his bedroom and shrugged into a periwinkle-blue button-down dress shirt and pulled on a pair of dark-wash jeans.

He slipped into a pair of deck shoes. Then he grabbed his keys off the counter by the front door, didn't bother to lock it, and got into his late-model Lexus.

He headed downtown to Piatto's Pizzeria. But he circled the block three times without finding a parking spot—a sure sign of tourist season on the island. He grinned.

He finally found a parking place along Queen Street when a minivan with Iowa plates pulled out of a spot.

Nathan walked along the red brick sidewalk. He nodded hello to the people he passed. Mostly, in early August, tourists with cameras slung around their necks.

The sounds of clicking silverware and people laughing drifted to him.

He caught the scent of oven-baked pizza and sun-warmed petunias as he strode up to the bright red wooden door of the pizzeria.

He was just about to pull it open when he heard a voice behind him.

"Hi, how are ya, Nathan?"

Nathan turned in the doorway to see a thin bald man in a blue windbreaker, with even bluer eyes. "Robert. Good, good. And you?"

"I'm fine. But I hear a congratulations is

in order."

Nathan moved aside and opened the old wooden door wider so a Japanese couple could go inside.

The older man continued, "That's no small feat, winning the Premier's Award for your design of the new Charlottetown Girl Guides site. Great work."

Nathan smiled. "Thanks. It was a fun and challenging side project." His gut tightened.

It was great. He enjoyed what he did. And after all the time and money he'd put in to getting his double degree, he should.

And yet... He fiddled with the hem of his untucked button-down. Something was missing. What, exactly, he wasn't quite sure...

But he set those thoughts aside. "You've done pretty well for yourself, too, Robert. Getting elected to deputy mayor."

The other man grinned. "Thanks. I feel I can do a lot of good for this city."

"I'm sure you can," Nathan replied and clapped the older man on the shoulder.

"Well, I'm off to the post office. But congratulations again. And if you ever come by city hall, the coffee's on me." Robert winked and then continued down the street.

Nathan's gaze darted inside the airy restaurant with its copper-plate ceiling and large windows along the front.

He spotted a slender blonde woman who sat by herself at a table near the door. That must be... What was her name? Oh, right. Vanessa. He should've remembered that.

He walked over to her, cleared his throat, and extended his hand. "Hi, how are ya?"

She grinned up at him, then got up and gave him a hug that lingered a few seconds. "Really good."

Nathan took a step back. "That's great." He picked up a menu as he sat down. "Decided on what I can get you for lunch?"

"Hmmm." She studied him over the edge of her menu. "I think I'll have their Salsiccia con Gorgonzola pizza. Would you like to share?"

"Uh, sure." Then he ordered a coffee. Black. Well, she was cute but he preferred brunettes.

"So," he said after he placed their order and leaned his arm against the table, "have you been here long?"

"Depends on what you mean by 'long.'" She laughed. Scooted closer. "I'm a born and raised Islander, if that's what you mean. But I've been here at Piatto's," she glanced at her watch, "about ten minutes so far. You?"

"Well, I'm a native Islander too. And I only just got here."

She laughed again. "I knew that." She touched his arm for a second. "So," she tucked a strand of already-neat hair behind her ear, "what high school did you go to, then?"

Their orders arrived before he could answer.

He fiddled with the coffee stir stick even though he never added cream or sugar. Then took a slice of pizza and bit into it.

After finishing the piece, Nathan again stirred his coffee that didn't need stirring. He glanced out the window in time to see a man in a tricorn hat consult a pocket watch as he crossed the street toward Cross Keys Condos. Must be one of the costumed Confederation Players doing a tour.

Nathan glanced down at his coffee cup. Looked out the window again. Blinked. The man was gone. He looked around. Had the Confederation Players changed their outfits from the 1860s to the 1770s? Nathan frowned. He probably just hadn't gotten enough sleep.

"Nathan?"

"Oh! Sorry. Um, it was Colonel Grey High."

Vanessa darted a glance his way over the rim of her water glass. "Colonel Grey, huh?" She took a sip then blinked up at him, her eyes wide, her lips slightly parted.

He shifted in his seat. "And you?"

"Oh, I went to Charlottetown Rural." She started digging through her purse. Took out her business card and handed it to him. "I'm free tonight." She paused. Looked up at him. Lowered her voice. "That is, if you are?"

Nathan felt a wave of disappointment wash through him. "Vanessa," he said. "You seem really nice. And you're cute. But...I can't go on any more dates with you. I'm just not that interested. I'm sorry."

"AND SO THEN," the 30-something man across the table from Ruby waved his fork, "I got the supervisor award. For the third year in a row. Plus, I got a fifty percent pay raise and a company car." He leaned forward. "A Mercedes. S Class." He grinned, and Ruby could see a slight gap between his front teeth. But the dimple in his cheek was rather appealing.

She fiddled with the stem of her wine glass. "Oh, that's, uh, great for you."

The man nodded. "Thanks!" He took a bite of his salmon.

Silence stretched between them. Ruby's mind strayed back to the love letter fragment. Such a romantic phrase: *the compass of the heart points in new directions*...No one talked like that any more. Least of all, to her...

Ruby placed her unused knife neatly on the edge of her plate. Then moved the wine glass from one side of the table to the other.

As if suddenly realizing she was still sitting there, the man said, "So, what is it that you do?"

"I'm currently a doctoral student for Simmons College. My focus is archival and preservation studies. I want to become a special collections librarian." Hmmm. But who wrote that romantic phrase? Whoever it was must have had a poet's soul...And did Edwina know it? Appreciate it? Return the sender's affections just as ardently? *Ardently*? What? She shook her head. She'd been reading so many antique documents that she'd started to think like that.

The man took another bite of his salmon. "Don't you like your job?"

"Oh! Yes. I love it—to me, discovering antique documents is like a treasure hunt." Hmmm. Would Dr. O'Neil's papers provide any new connections between Edwina and whoever she was receiving letters from?

"That's great. So what are you working on now?"

"Well," Ruby said, and made a wry face. "I was running late to this date, actually, because I was researching. So I actually have a few photocopies here." She paged through her notes. She came to her copy of Washington's signed orders Dr. O'Neil had sent her, and handed the first one to her date.

Headquarters   October 16, 1775

...Should you meet with any vessel, the property of the inhabitants of Canada, not employed in any respect in the service of the ministerial army, you are to treat such vessel with all kindness, and by no means suffer them to be injured or molested.

George Washington

He glanced up at her as he finished

reading, a questioning look on his face.

"Oh, I'm not really concerned about George Washington. I'm hoping that I'll be able to find out more about a woman named Edwina Belliveaux, who actually isn't mentioned in that."

Her date frowned. "So why do you have this one?"

"Since I'm researching love letters, and not George Washington, I only have this order because it's one link in the paper trail that I'm hoping will lead me to more information about Edwina. She's the subject of a fragment that I'm wanting to use in my research on women's love letters in the American Revolution."

"Oh. Well, that's...great. And where is this Edwina mentioned?"

"In a different document. I have it right here, actually." Ruby handed him the other printout from Dr. O'Neil's emails.

Headquarters   November 25, 1775

Now that Captains Selman and Broughton have been dealt with and their ranks stripped from them, you are to send Miss Belliveaux back to the Island of St. John and Charlotte Town at once.

Though she has done a great dis-

service by being under my employ as a so-called privateer, and in truth, disobeyed the earlier direct order from me after having set sail for Charlotte Town, now that the true loyalties of Edwina Belliveaux have been discovered to lie not with the Crown nor the Patriots, but with those of Acadian descent, you are not to harm her.

While she has not persuaded the French-Canadians to be favorable to our Patriot cause, as I had hoped she might, let the Loyalists in Canada seal her fate. Her blood shall not be upon the hands of the Patriots.

George Washington

"So what was the connection, exactly, between Washington's second order and the love letter fragment?" her date asked.

Ruby leaned forward. "That question had been going through my head ever since I started corresponding with a professor in Canada eight months ago. It seems pretty clear that the Edwina in the love letter was the same Edwina who appeared in this order."

"Well, sounds like a fascinating mystery for you." He handed back the photo-copies. Straightened his tie. "So. Did I tell you about the time I went scuba diving in Bora Bora?"

Ruby fought down a surge of disappointment. Why had she expected him, even for a moment, to be as excited as she was about this?

She flicked her eyes to her watch. What would she find when she went through Dr. O'Neil's papers? Ruby had already been in touch with Evie, Dr. O'Neil's daughter. She'd said Ruby would be welcome to stay in her dad's now-unused place at Cross Keys Condos downtown. So her accommodations were taken care of. Now she just had to pack.

As Ruby's date looked down at his plate and took the last bites of his meal, she cocked her head. From this angle, his jawline looked appealing. She squinted, and decided that it pretty much cancelled out the fact that his hairline had started to recede.

No. A man's hairline had nothing to do with his character. She had to look past that.

A few minutes later, the waiter arrived with the check. Would he want to split it like the last guy had?

Ruby's date smiled at her. "My treat." He took the bill and paid in cash. "Are you all set?"

Ruby nodded.

"Can I walk you to your car?"

"...Sure."

He held open the restaurant door for Ruby and they walked out into the cool summer evening.

"Well," he said, as they came to a stop in front of Ruby's black Toyota sedan, "I had a nice time. Let's do this again sometime."

Ruby's smile faltered but she reached for polite words. "Thanks for dinner and uh, that sounds...nice."

He opened the driver's door for her and then headed off to his own car. Ruby got in and drove back to her apartment.

This guy was nice enough. Had paid for their meal. Even if he did tend to talk a bit too much about himself. Maybe it didn't matter that he hadn't asked her any follow-up questions about herself. And he was decent looking...

She withheld a sigh. She couldn't expect more than that. What did it say about her love life that the only thing that got her pulse to race these days was a centuries-old love letter? And not even a whole one, at that?

She shook the thoughts off, unlocked her apartment and let herself in. Time to pack for Charlottetown.

She walked into her bedroom, pulled out her battered flowered purple suitcase, and unzipped it.

First, though, she should probably change out of her work clothes and into something more comfortable.

She slipped off her blouse and slid out of her slim gray trousers. She folded them and put them away in her dresser drawer before she realized she still had her jewelry on.

She took out her rhinestone earrings and slipped off her imitation Cartier watch. Then she pulled on her favorite jeans and blue tank top, careful to lift up the locket to avoid its chain catching in the knit fabric.

As she settled the locket back into place, she slid her fingers around the cool sterling silver etched with tiny flowers.

Out of habit, she flicked it open. On the left, a miniature painting of a handsome dark-haired man with brown eyes looked back at her, his hair neatly tied in a queue. On the right, a miniature painting of a beautiful woman with green eyes and blonde hair in neat ringlets. Ruby smiled. Who were these people? She had to admit, she loved to speculate about it ever since she'd picked the locket up at that flea market in the North End.

She noticed the picture of the man had somehow gotten a bit off-center, so she moved a fingertip to adjust it. Hmmm. That didn't work.

She unfastened the locket. She held it in both hands and tried to get a better angle to adjust the picture. Well, maybe it'd be easier to take it out and slide it all the way back in again.

She gently tugged on the thick antique paper. It came out easily. But behind the miniature was a small square of folded paper. Ruby cocked her head. She put the locket down then unfolded the small square:

> *Cardinal directions of the heart*
> *Impart the way toward True North*
> *Good-hearted General's Orders did put forth;*
> *Crowned Head of Justice, strong and brave*
> *Cradled on the wind and waves*

Huh. What was this? How had it gotten in there? She readjusted the miniature and put it back into place, now centered then snapped the locket shut.

Cardinal directions of the heart... Why did that sound so familiar?

She'd have to look at it more closely after she'd finished packing. Could it be some sort of poem? Or possibly a rhyme? Or...she grinned. A riddle?

She pushed up her glasses. Nah. Nothing that exciting ever happened to her. She turned back to her packing.

AS NATHAN STRODE back to his car after his failed date, he unwrapped a white chocolate Hershey bar—the last portion of his lunch—and took a bite. But the sweetness of his favorite chocolate brought up a bitter memory.

He and Dad had been in the study, had that argument... He sighed and his mouth tightened. The last one they'd had before he'd died in February. Was that really six months ago?

And now he couldn't take it back. Couldn't say, "I'm sorry," and then swipe the white chocolate Hershey bar from Dad's desk drawer to offer him half.

His lips rose in a crooked half-smile. But it faded. Now both of his parents were gone...

"Are you even listening to what I'm saying, Nathan? You can't just loaf around here like some teenager or homeless person."

Nathan had crossed his arms and hunched his shoulders, but kept his voice calm. Rational. "Dad. I got fired. It's not the end of the world. Just because jobs are hard to come by here on Prince Edward Island doesn't mean that I won't get another one. Statistically speaking—"

"Quite being so damn logical, Nathan." Dr. Gordon O'Neil's voice grew louder. "Sometimes life is more than numbers and statistics. Sometimes you have to let that go and figure out what you want to do with your life. You can't just keep working these dead-end jobs. You need to actually use your graphic design degree—"

Nathan had taken a bite of the chocolate and clenched his fists. "I'm 33 years old, Dad. Please don't talk to me like I'm 17."

"I'm still your father."

"Sometimes I wonder."

"What's that supposed to mean?"

"It means that on this island, family is the most important thing. Roots. Connections."

"Yes, well, you'd better start exercising some of those connections or you'll be working at God knows where—McDonald's—

the rest of your life!" A vein ticked in Dr. O'Neil's temple.

"Calm down, Dad. You know what the doctor said."

"I won't calm down. I need to make this point to you! Can't you see? I'm on your case because I care about you. Your future. You're not going to be the only O'Neil on Prince Edward Island who's failed."

Nathan had snapped off another piece of chocolate and chewed furiously. "Just because this family has roots in this place going back to 1768, doesn't mean I have to be like every last one of them!"

"Yes, well, you've already proven that quite nicely now, haven't you?"

"Dad." Nathan had raked a hand through his hair, fought down the surge of anger. "You know I love you. But should you really be the one to talk? Everyone thinks your theories about the Great Seal are, well, crazy... Even I think that and I know how much work you've put into them. And let's not even talk about your ridiculous ideas about the seal being part of some sort of treasure."

"Good idea. Let's not talk about that. Because finding the lost seal isn't the point of this discussion, son. Though I do have reason to believe I'm about to find it."

"You can't find it, Dad. That's impossible. It was melted down for bullets long ago. And there is no treasure, either. You should realize that and stop wasting your life on—"

"Wasting my life?" Dr. O'Neil raised his brows. "At least I'm using my education. At least I'm making something of myself."

"Thanks, Dad." Nathan had blinked rapidly. But then his blue eyes, the exact shade of his father's, flashed. "Just because I made a few mistakes, took a few risks in university, doesn't mean I'm only capable of being the black sheep you seem to think I am."

"So that means those broken engagements, that pot smoking, and those reckless driving tickets mean nothing?"

Nathan had hunched his shoulders. "I only broke off two engagements. And I don't smoke pot any more. People can change."

Dr. O'Neil had opened his mouth to reply but sagged against his desk instead, and let his head drop to his chest.

Nathan's heart felt squeezed in a vise. "Dad?" He touched a hand to his father's shoulder.

"I'm fine." Dr. O'Neil shook off his son's concern. "Just a little...out of breath."

Nathan suddenly hadn't been able to catch his own breath. "All right, Dad," he had said softly, "if it means that much to you, I'll start looking for something else right away."

Dr. O'Neil had straightened up. Nathan's shoulders had relaxed. "One of my buddies from uni works at a software company here in Charlottetown. Maybe they need a graphic design guy."

A seagull wheeled and called overhead. Nathan blinked away the memory and took a deep breath. He crumpled up the empty Hersey wrapper and tossed it into the trash can. He wished he could toss out the guilt and regret just as easily. Because now he'd never have the chance to make things right.

Chapter Two

NATHAN SHRUGGED OUT of his green jacket and slung it over the back of the antique Windsor chair in the cream-tiled hallway of the split-level he'd inherited from his grandma.

This evening, he could transpose bits and pieces of the initial sketch he'd done at Fort Amherst onto a larger piece of real drawing paper.

He went to the fridge and fished out the last bottle of Beach Chair Lager behind a carton of Chinese takeout and headed out the screened-in back porch.

He inhaled the scent of freshly mowed grass from his neighbor's yard. He took a seat on the old wicker porch swing, its faded blue gingham pillows ones his grandma had stitched from her mother's rag bag.

His lips lifted in a half-smile. Another Island trait—mending and making do.

He leaned back against the pillows. Took a sip of his beer. A light breeze played across his face and carried with it the scent of impending summer rain.

His mind returned to his date earlier in the day.

People around here liked to think he was a heartbreaker. And it was true.

He raked a hand through his hair. But that had never stopped women from throwing themselves at him.

A fact he wasn't proud of. In fact, he'd broken the heart of his most recent ex when he'd walked away after six months.

She'd asked him to be her boyfriend after the fourth date.

So he'd stayed. Because he had hoped his feelings would change. Grow into something...more...than what they were.

But it just became six months of emptiness. At least, for him. But for her, it'd become six months in which she'd grown to love him so much that she'd basically proposed marriage one night as they lay in the dark of his bedroom.

Somehow, you could say things in the pitch black that you couldn't quite find the courage for in the light of dawn.

He never should've let it go on that long. It really wasn't fair. To either of them. He sighed. He shouldn't be this dissatisfied in his love life. It didn't make any sense. Wasn't that the nature of love, anyway? To make compromises? To be a bit...disappointed?

Because the whole notion of true love was just a fiction. People were happy enough together. Could even have fulfilling, satisfying lives together if they simply liked each other. Right? Of course they could. It happened all the time.

He took another sip of beer.

Then why didn't that seem like enough, for him? As irrational as that sounded.

He pushed aside his negative thoughts and got to his feet. He drained the rest of the beer and tossed the empty bottle into the blue recycle bin by the back door.

In the kitchen, he had just flicked on the dishwasher when he heard a rumble of thunder. All at once, it was pouring rain.

The rain beat down on the roof. Outside, treetops bent in the force of the wind.

Cold and wet blew through the kitchen, and Nathan shut the window just in time.

He dashed around the rest of the house to make sure no windows were left open. He eased the small leather-bound book out of his back pocket and placed it in a half-empty drawer of his nightstand. He'd look at it later.

But that's when he remembered he'd left the window to his dad's office open earlier that day after he and his sister had gone over there to consult with the contractor for some renovations.

He dashed out the door and across the lawn to his car. It wasn't that far to the condo. The rain started to filter through his heather-green cotton V-neck T-shirt during the short sprint to the car. He sped over to the condo but didn't bother to roll up the car windows as he drove.

As he pulled into the lot, the rain came down in sheets. Well, the secondary entrance was closer. He jumped out of the car, reached the building's back door and pressed down on the brass thumb latch of the curved door handle. It didn't budge.

He could feel his shirt start to stick to his back as the rain pelted down.

He searched his jeans pockets for the key. It wasn't there.

Damn.

He jogged back over to his car, his shirt now pretty much soaked through.

He shook the water out of his eyes and grabbed the right key ring after he fished around a minute or two in the jumble of odds and ends in his console.

He ran back across the parking lot and then the sidewalk. It took him three tries but finally he fit the key into the lock.

He shook his head at himself. He was usually better at this. Well, maybe that was only when he was unhooking a woman's bra with one hand.

Not that he'd done that in awhile...

AS THE AIR Canada jet angled a little to the left to circle the Charlottetown airport, Ruby peered out the small window. Late afternoon sunlight sparkled on the blue Northumberland Strait. Patches of gray rainclouds interlaced with the dark green of pine trees and the lighter green of rolling hills. Even from this height, she could see red sandstone cliffs topped with bright green grass. The surf curled and ebbed against the uneven shoreline of the island.

The plane touched down. Ruby's pulse thudded in her throat.

What if Dr. O'Neil's papers didn't contain any more of the information she needed? What if she was completely wasting her time and this didn't make any difference in qualifying her for the position? What if she'd have to re-do her whole 300-page dissertation?

She shook her head. Lifted her chin. It wouldn't come to that.

"Ladies and gentlemen," the flight attendant said, "it'll just be a second while the ground crew brings around the stairs. No skybridge at this airport. Please watch your step as you go down."

After a few minutes, the fasten seatbelt sign dinged off, and Ruby stood.

She made her way down the steps of the airplane. The afternoon sunshine glinted gold off the metal of the airplane and tinged the expanse of sky. As Ruby crossed the tarmac, a fine mist of rain started to fall.

With the rain came the scent of salt air and she inhaled. A smile spread slowly across her face.

Was it her imagination or did the ocean smell different here than in Massachusetts? She closed her eyes. She could almost imagine herself walking through a pine forest, carrying a woven basket filled with bread. The fine cotton of her green-striped summer dress swished around her, the sounds of the surf off to her left as seagulls called and wheeled overhead.

A wave of longing and homesickness

surged through her. A seagull called again, and she startled. Her eyes opened.

What? How could she feel homesick for this place when she'd only just arrived? Besides, she'd grown up in the city.

She frowned and shook away the feeling. Where had that come from? But she shrugged. Just due to the time difference, that's all. She yawned. And the long trip.

A *Welcome to Prince Edward Island* sign caught her eye as she walked through the sliding glass door to the tiny arrivals area.

As Ruby headed to the baggage carousel, she looked around. On her left, displays showed photos of rolling green hills and fields of blooming pink lupine. Other images depicted smiling children who dug clams on the beach. The wet red sand squished between their toes. More pictures illustrated laughing couples seated on outdoor patios with red-brick paving stones and old-fashioned lampposts.

A sense of lightness filled Ruby's chest, and her heart beat faster.

She retrieved her overstuffed purple flowered suitcase from the baggage carousel. But as she set it down, it wobbled and pitched over.

She righted it and noticed that one of its wheels had snapped off. Well, the suitcase was old. And baggage handlers could be a little rough on luggage. She dragged the damaged suitcase along and headed out the arrivals door as the rain began to fall harder.

NATHAN TOOK THE stairs to the fourth floor and stepped inside number 415. He shut the door quickly behind him and heaved a sigh of relief.

Until he realized he had dripped water all over the faded Oriental rug in the foyer.

He took off his leather flip-flops and wiped his feet before he went into the bathroom and rooted around for a towel.

Nothing.

A knot settled into his stomach and his fingers clenched. As he closed the linen closet door, he caught the familiar scent of Downy as he did.

He swallowed.

Water settled around his bare feet and he headed into the kitchen to grab a dishtowel.

The tea towel drawer squeaked on its runners. It'd been doing that for as long as he could remember: the sound of child-hood. He gave the drawer a pat as he shut it.

After he towelled off his hair with a faded tea towel printed with lavender sprigs, he shoved the towel into his back pocket and shut the window over the sink.

The rain pounded on the roof.

The wind suddenly shifted and began to keen through the open living room windows. He darted over to shut both of them, then turned and started down the hall.

His footsteps slowed, though, as he approached the first door on the left.

With his lips pressed together, he pushed open the door and got a whiff of cherry tobacco and leather-bound books.

He stood there for a second and looked at the mess.

Overfull boxes piled on top of drawers piled on top of accordion file-folders, which bulged at the seams, full of every sort of scrap of paper, newspaper clipping and online article printout.

If a messy desk was a sign of genius, then his dad must have truly been an Einstein of his field.

RUBY DASHED TO the nearest cab. The driver rolled down his window. "I've got another fare heading downtown, but you can hop in if you're headed there too."

Ruby nodded, and the man got out to stow her luggage.

"How are ya?" he said, as Ruby got in. "Where you headed?"

"Cross Keys Condos, please."

The man pulled into traffic. "So where you from?" he said.

"Boston."

"Ah," the man grinned, and the bobble-headed yellow duck on the dash seemed to grin, too. "Got a few cousins down that way. Haven't been there myself, though. What's your name?"

"Ruby." Ruby glanced out the window as the car turned on to North River Road and dropped off the first fare. It was pouring rain now. "Zalonski," she added.

"Hmmm. Can't say I know that last name."

"No, it's not too common. It's my adoptive last name."

The man nodded, and so did the yellow duck on the dash. "My wife's adopted. Can't imagine not knowing who your father is, myself, though. How long you in town for?"

A wrought iron fence surrounded one brightly painted blue house with red geraniums that hung in baskets on the wide white porch.

"About a week," Ruby answered. "I'm hoping to make this a fairly quick trip—I have a dissertation to defend back in Boston soon. But I'm here on university business. Cataloging some papers." She turned her head and saw a weathered gray clapboard house, shaded by broad leafy oaks and maples.

The cab slowed and turned right onto Euston Street. They passed a three-story red brick home. It had white columns and what must be a 300-year-old oak tree in the yard, with roots that almost spilled out onto the street.

But the car kept going.

More houses. More big trees. Ruby grinned. She couldn't help but remember the big oak that her adoptive father had hung a rope swing from. She'd spent every second that she could, during her childhood summers, outside in that big swing.

The taxi turned onto Queen Street. "Here we are." The driver pulled into a parking spot in front of a four-story red brick building with a bronze plaque affixed to it. Ruby noticed the date—1773.

A bistro called Terre Rouge shared the first floor with a gourmet olive oil store.

Baskets of pink and purple petunias hung from old-fashioned cast iron lamp-posts.

The driver got out and pulled Ruby's suitcase out of the back. Ruby got out too. She pulled up the hood of her light summer jacket, and paid the driver. She made sure to tip him.

"Have a good one. The condo's around to the side there," he said, as he pointed to Ruby's right, before he drove away.

Ruby sprinted around the corner. She pulled her battered suitcase behind her and opened the door of the condo entrance. She noticed the hand-painted, gold-lettered, wooden sign with two old-fashioned brass keys overlapping one another. She'd arrived at Cross Keys Condos.

In the lobby, a large carriage-lantern hung overhead, which threw the marble floor into a flattering, mellow light. Ruby punched the code that Evie had given her into the keypad by the door. She let herself into the foyer before she pressed the call button on the elevator.

NATHAN COULDN'T HELP glancing at the

Globe & Mail article documenting his father's discovery of yet another elusive historical tidbit about some famous dead person.

Like Edwina Belliveaux. Nathan reached out and automatically straightened the framed yellowed newspaper clipping on the right-hand corner of the desk. It had been there for as long as he could remember. He picked it up:

> *One of the island's most recognizable forebearers, Edwina Belliveaux, gets yet another honorable mention today, as a plaque with her name on it has been installed—*

God. He blinked rapidly and set the framed clipping down. Now that famous dead person was his own father. Nathan pressed his lips together and moved to the wall of windows opposite the roll-top desk.

Rain blew in and made circles of damp on the highly polished hardwood and the red-and-blue Aubusson rug. It filled his nose with the scent of damp wool and lemon floor wax.

He reached into his back pocket, pulled out the kitchen towel and began to mop up the mess.

It'd probably be easier if he shut the windows first, though. He got up from his crouch and moved to the window.

It stuck a bit, swollen slightly from the humidity and the rain.

He pushed harder. He'd just gotten the old six-by-six wavy glass to move down an inch when a loud banging sounded in the hallway.

Nathan crossed the study and stubbed his bare toe on the leg of an antique writing desk that sat by the room's entrance.

But he couldn't help smiling at it even though his toe throbbed. His mother had bought the Federal-style desk at an auction in Rustico. He ran a finger along its cherry-wood surface.

He'd always wondered about the series of notches on the underside of the writing surface. Who had owned it?

More banging.

He made his way to the front entrance and put his hand on the doorknob just as his skin broke out in goose bumps.

He shook it off and opened the door. No one was there. A sense of déja vù coursed through him.

He paused but then leaned out further into the hall.

A young woman stood in the hallway with her back to him as she tried to lift a heavy-looking suitcase. One of its wheels, he noticed, had sheered off completely. She struggled up the stairs.

He took a step out into the hall. But before he could offer help, she'd lugged the suitcase over the final stair step. She spun around. Her eyes widened behind her glasses as she realized someone else was in the hallway.

He met her gaze. The hairs on the back of his neck stood up as the sharp tang of sea salt and the sweetness of wild roses filled his senses.

His throat constricted. He cleared it. That was quite the perfume. Shampoo. Or—hand lotion?

A sting of tears prickled his eyes as he continued to hold her hazel gaze.

He tried to force himself to look away. But couldn't.

The blood pounded in his veins, and he felt as if he'd just jumped off a cliff. A sharp, sweet sort of joy clutched at his heart while regret and longing rose within him. His throat worked. Two words, deep and resonant, coursed through his heart and mind—*I'm sorry*.

What?

He held his breath. Frowned. What *were* all these emotions? Nothing. He blinked away the sting of tears.

He was probably just tired. He actually hadn't slept well the past few nights. Yet he found he couldn't speak.

He watched, wordless, as she took a step backward while her lips formed an O. But no words came out of her mouth, either.

He cleared his throat again. Finally managed, "Don't go." Huh? He swallowed. Chuckled and rubbed a hand across the back of his neck then said, "I mean, can I help you?"

She shook her head, and her glossy blonde curls shimmied and fell in shining waves down the smooth satiny skin of her bare back—He blinked. No. That didn't make any sense.

Her hair was in a ponytail. Yes. She had brown hair, not blonde. Right. And she was wearing a yellow T-shirt. She took a shaky breath. "Y-yes. I'm looking for Dr. Gordon O'Neil's condo."

His fingers gripped the doorframe. He couldn't stop staring at her. As if he'd never get his fill. As if, when he blinked, she might disappear. What? That was ridiculous. Of course she wouldn't disappear. "This is it."

The young woman shifted the bag to her other hand. "Well, his daughter Evie told me I could come by."

"My sister?" Nathan shifted his weight. Forced himself to concentrate. "I hadn't heard anything about that."

"Oh. And who are you?" The woman lifted her chin.

"I'm, uh," he riffled a hand through his damp hair. Frowned. "Dr. O'Neil's son. Nathan."

"Oh," the young woman repeated. Crossed her arms. "Well, can you please let me inside? My name's Ruby Zalonski. And I've come to catalog his papers."

RUBY WAS NOT going to stare at the way Nathan's rain-soaked heather-green cotton T-shirt clung to the contours of his chest. She had important work to do. Or how something in his gaze seemed to speak of moonlit beaches, wild roses and second chances.

She frowned. Huh?

He looked like he'd just stepped from a movie set: ripped jeans, tousled black hair, soaked T-shirt and all. Her heart leapt to her throat. How could anyone this gorgeous be for real?

Well, she was smarter than to get carried away by something like good looks. Looks didn't tell you anything. Evie's warning about her brother's reputation told her everything. She straightened her spine. Pushed up her glasses.

"What's this about?" Nathan's eyes narrowed, and as he tilted his head, a few strands of his damp, dark hair fell across his forehead.

Ruby lifted her chin though her heart raced. She couldn't help staring at those stray strands of thick dark hair.

She shoved her hands into the pockets of her white capris so that she wouldn't smooth away the stray strands for him. "For my doctoral dissertation. I'm from Simmons College and I'd arranged to catalog Dr. O'Neil's papers for—"

"Well, I have no idea what you're talking about." Nathan started to close the door.

"Wait," Ruby said, and put her hand on the doorframe near his. "Your sister told me I could stay here. Now that...now that there's an unused bedroom?"

Nathan's gaze flicked down at the suitcase at her feet. Something about the way his lashes rested on his cheekbones as he glanced down at her suitcase had a fierce sadness washing through her. Like she'd gotten here too late. That she'd missed her chance—

His gaze flicked back up to her. Held.

She caught her breath.

He blinked. "Uh, come in for now." He paused. "I'll just confirm with Evie in a bit."

"Thank you," she managed around the lump that suddenly lodged in her throat. She took a breath. Cleared her throat.

Saw him swallow. "You're welcome." A beat of silence. "Here, let me take that." He leaned forward to take her broken suitcase and she watched the cotton of his T-shirt stretch across his bicep as he picked up the luggage.

Ruby forced herself to take a deep breath. Then she followed him inside as he turned and shut the door to the condo behind them.

"Watch yourself," Nathan said, "it's a bit messy in here. Renovations."

She bent her head and slipped off her faux alligator-print wedges.

A quick look around revealed a short hallway with a gold-and-cream Oriental rug. It was only then she noticed his feet were bare, too. She felt her cheeks turn pink.

She curled her toes into the thick wool as she saw his broad shoulders tense underneath his shirt when he turned to glance over his shoulder.

In reply to the unspoken question in his gaze, she followed him down the short hallway. When she looked to the left, she saw what he meant.

Ladders and paint cans were strewn around, and a big plastic drop sheet covered the flooring. Long sheets of drywall leaned against the exposed-brick walls, and big plastic trashcans were heaped up with plaster and lathe.

"That must have been the living room?"

"Yep. We're having it redone. The roof started to leak awhile back, and up here on the top floor, it somehow went unnoticed."

He stopped suddenly at a door on the right. He pressed his palm to the smooth surface of the burnished wooden door and pushed it open. Ruby felt a shiver go up her spine as she watched his fingertips caress the wood. She peered inside.

It was a study—and a complete mess.

"Dad had his own filing system, if you could call it that. Only another academic could figure it out. If they had a lucky day."

Which, she was rapidly discovering, wasn't today for her.

NATHAN PUSHED AWAY from the doorframe and shoved aside the strange sensations and irrational emotions as he did so. Those feelings didn't make any sense. Therefore, he wasn't going to pay any attention to them. He had to deal with what was in front of him.

And right now, it was this woman.

"So you're here to catalog my dad's papers?"

She passed him on the threshold. He had to shove his hands in his jeans pockets to stop himself from reaching out to smooth back the stray strand that had come loose from her ponytail.

"Yes. But don't worry, they've only sent me here for a week. Academic budgets, and all that."

He mentally shook his head. Took a deep breath and let it out slowly. She wanted to catalog Dad's things. That meant she was going to be here in the middle of these renovations.

"Wait. Wait."

She paused. Turned her head to look

at him.

"Where did you say you were from, again?"

"People ask that a lot around here." Ruby laughed lightly and tucked the stray strand of hair behind her ear. "Boston. Simmons College." She cleared her throat and shifted from foot to foot.

This woman was an outsider. From away. He winced inwardly. He'd always disliked that term, 'from away.' He wasn't of his grandfather's generation. He shouldn't feel any sort of suspicion or distrust for her just because she was from off-island.

He crossed his arms. Studied her unruly brunette waves, her tortoiseshell glasses, and the yellow cotton T-shirt that fit her so perfectly.

He swallowed. But how could he trust this tidal wave of emotions she'd plunged him into, just by...just by standing in front of him?

And if she was from away, then why did it feel so good to have her here? "So you're an academic too."

Ruby put her hand on her hip. "Not yet. But I soon will be. I'm working on my doctorate."

"That wouldn't happen to be a doctorate in P.E.I. history, would it?"

Ruby frowned and crossed her arms. "No. It's in archival studies, actually."

"But you were corresponding with my father."

"...Yes."

"Let me guess." He also crossed his arms. "You probably think the lost seal can be found too. And that Edwina Belliveaux had something more to do with it than what history says."

"You know," Ruby said as she un-shouldered her carry-on and set it down by her bare feet. Nathan saw the polish she'd used was a pale pink. "Some people happen to think your father's work was revolutionary."

She held his gaze. Continued. "He wasn't afraid to stand up for what he believed in, no matter what other people thought. No matter what other people said."

"Well, those other people had plenty to say." Nathan frowned and regarded her.

She didn't break eye contact. "They thought he was crazy. A crackpot. All his conspiracy theories about the Great Seal, the pounds sterling and that 'famous quote'"—Ruby made air quotes with her fingers—"from Edwina."

"Exactly. So I wouldn't waste my time if I were you. That's what got him his reputation in the first place." Nathan raised his eyebrows at the memory. "He seemed to think the lost seal meant something more than what everyone thought." He shook his head. "And that Edwina stole it instead of trying to save it."

She continued as if she hadn't heard him. "That's why we started corresponding in the first place." She crouched beside her carry-on. Took out a glossy black leather folder, which, Nathan saw, contained a brand new legal pad, a freshly sharpened No. 2 pencil, and an array of rainbow-hued sticky notes.

Nathan waved a hand in the general direction of the mess. "Well, I'll save you the trouble of sifting through all these—"

"—valuable resources?" She straightened up. And the glance she shot him held just enough fierceness that he lifted his palms.

Ruby flicked a page in the legal pad over to a clean sheet then picked up the pencil and licked the tip. God. His gut tightened. What the hell was happening to him?

He watched her jot the date, and—she glanced at her watch—the time, onto the page in neat, curving script.

Nathan shifted to lean back against the glass top of his father's massive oak desk. "Don't tell me you're here to *find* the Great Seal? Chase down some ridiculous notion about a treasure?"

Ruby raised her brows. "And if I was?"

Nathan shook his head and opened his mouth.

"For your information," Ruby said, and crossed her arms again, "I'm here to catalog his papers, not make judgements. My research is focused on love letters. I'm hoping to find out more about one particular love letter, actually. One that Edwina received from...someone." The color rose on her cheeks. "I want to figure out just who. And if there's something in your dad's papers that can help me, so much the better."

"You like that, don't you?" Nathan said. He rested his hands, palm down, against the smooth glass-topped surface of the desk. He studied Ruby, his head cocked. "The romance of it all..." He rubbed one hand up and down his opposite arm.

"There's nothing wrong with that." Ruby shot him a look filled with annoyance.

"Love letter research?" Nathan tugged

at his earlobe. "Isn't that a little..." He shrugged, rubbed the back of his neck. "I don't know—"

"No." Ruby frowned. "That's right. You *don't* know. This is my research, not yours." She tapped her foot. "I thought Canadians were supposed to be polite."

"Don't believe everything you hear."

Chapter Three

RUBY'S GRIP TIGHTENED on the plastic grocery bags. It had finally stopped raining. She carried her bags down Queen Street toward Cross Keys Condos later that evening as she dodged puddles.

She walked through tree-lined Victoria Row, with its paving bricks, brightly colored picnic benches, and white fairy lights strung between leafy tree limbs.

But it wasn't the sound of the live jazz band playing on the outdoor stage that caught her ear, but Nathan's name.

She turned her head, and spotted two older women seated at a bright yellow picnic table under a maple tree.

"That Nathan O'Neil, I heard he broke up with yet another one just the other day. And after only the first date. Are these Island girls not good enough for him?" The woman shook her head.

Ruby paused mid-stride.

"That man never changes," said the other woman. "He's 33 and still acts like a teenager. At least he quit smoking pot. But he's still breaking hearts at every turn. One day he'll wake up and realize he's thrown his life away. Old and lonely, I tell you."

Ruby's eyes widened, and she strained to catch their words. Was that true? The tiniest bit of disappointment made her stomach dip. But then she shook her head at herself. Evie had warned her about Nathan's reputation... Yet why had she had such strong emotions around him?

"But all the women run to him. Girls these days have no sense to let a man do the chasing." The other woman clucked her tongue.

The first woman nodded. "Hard to believe he's an O'Neil. Who would break off two engagements?—not like any of his ancestors, that's sure."

Two engagements? No. Ruby lifted her chin. She shouldn't just stand here and listen to idle gossip. It wasn't right. And it wasn't true.

"Shame about what happened up at UPEI with his dad. Too bad the poor man had to pass away so suddenly."

Although, *that* was definitely true...

"And did you hear? Apparently Nathan got a $300 ticket—talking on his phone and driving at the same time. He always was a bit of a reckless driver. I should know. My Marvin was his driver's ed teacher."

Ruby adjusted her grip on her grocery bags. She couldn't keep standing here, listening.

"Anyways, how was your doctor's appointment...?"

Their voices faded as Ruby walked on by. It was none of her business what kind of person Nathan was. After all, she was only here for a week. If he had a bit of a heartbreaker reputation, so what? It wasn't like he'd shown any interest in her.

And even if he had shown interest, she was smarter than to get involved. She'd only end things after the third date, what with her commitment issues, so the whole thing would be going nowhere from the start.

But Nathan's blue eyes flashed through her mind anyway.

NATHAN HEADED BACK to his own house after Ruby had gotten settled in at the condo, and ambled into the kitchen to make himself a sandwich.

Where had she come from, Ruby? Boston, she'd said. That was somewhere he'd never been. He hadn't been off-island except once, for a work conference in Toronto.

She'd probably been all over. Seen interesting people and places. And discovered all sorts of history...

His heart beat a little faster. He wanted to sit down and talk to her for hours. The conversations they could have. The places she could tell him about, and then that they could discover, together. Take it all in. Take her all in, gather her up in his arms...

He could just imagine her in a long skirt...She picked up the damp hem and laughed as she ran along the shore. The sunlight in her eyes. The expression on her face as she looked over her shoulder at him. The feel of her long legs, smooth and silky under his touch...His heart pounded. He blinked. Stared at the contents of his fridge.

Wait, what was he doing again? He tried to dislodge the errant images.

Right. Sandwich.

Nathan got the bread, meat and mayo from the fridge and set them on the counter. He gave a frustrated sigh. What was going on here? There had to be some logical explanation for it. Had to be.

Otherwise...

He slathered mayo on two pieces of Wonder Bread.

Otherwise—he shut his eyes, and all he could see was Ruby's hazel eyes. Looking back at him.

He shook his head. No doubt she was just like his father. Probably just as crazy as Dad, too. All that talk about love letters and research. He frowned. Who researched love letters?

He slapped a slice of turkey between the pieces of bread and carried the plate to his small dining room table.

He snorted. Next she'd want to run around and try to actually find the seal or something. He wasn't going to waste his time on any more thoughts about her. No matter how beautiful her hazel eyes had been.

Wide. Green flecked with golden brown. Deep and wise and rimmed with dark, long lashes that reflected an expression almost as startled as his own—What the hell was happening?

He ate the sandwich. Got up and put his dirty dishes into the dishwasher.

Shook his head. Shoved his hands

through his hair. No. No.

Otherwise—the only logical explanation would be—"Completely illogical.
Completely irrational. This has no ground-
ing in any sort of...sense."

And now he was talking to himself.

He had to go pick up the last of Dad's
papers from his office tomorrow and go
through the rest of Dad's stuff there.
Hmmm. Ruby would be there at the condo,
probably—maybe she'd be there when he
dropped them off? A grin snuck across
Nathan's face.

Which he immediately straightened
into a thin line.

The only logical explanation for this
was...lust. Of course. That was it.

The grin snuck onto his face again.

He crossed his arms. Pursed his lips.

No. He cocked his head. It was as if
he'd already known her forever, even
though he'd never met her before in his
life.

It was a knowing. *Beyond* knowing. It
was a rightness. A...a...Completely illogical
and crazy notion. He didn't feel anything
for her. Besides maybe a bit of attraction. A
bit of lust—

Buzz. Buzzzz.

Nathan jumped. Reached for his phone.

"Evie?"

"Nathan, hi. Listen, Ruby got there okay and everything, right?"

As Evie spoke, Nathan could hear the twins' whoops of glee in the background. *'Let's play post office! Grandpa said I got to keep his old paper. Here, now you can mail it.'*

"Girls," Evie's voice was muffled. "Mommy's on the phone. Shhh. Go in your room and play with the dollhouse."

Nathan smiled to himself as he leaned against the wall between the kitchen and living room. "Yeah, yeah, she got here just fine. I was going to call you in a bit and ask. Cuz I didn't know anything about it, so I was a bit...surprised."

"Sorry, Nathan. I meant to text you about it yesterday. But with the twins' new dance lessons starting and this bicentennial celebration documentation at work to organize..."

Nathan rubbed the back of his neck. "It's okay."

He heard Evie sigh with relief. "You're okay with her staying there, right? I know we're working with the contractor to do those renovations." Evie raised her voice as the dog barked and peals of laughter followed.

Nathan's heart clenched. Evie didn't have time to handle any of this. The least he could do was agree to help her out. "Evie, don't worry about it. I'll take care of everything."

A pause.

"You're sure? I mean, I know we agreed to do it all together. I can drop by if you need to..."

"No, no," Nathan said, his voice gentle. "You have far too much going on. I'll handle everything."

"Well...if you're sure you think you can."

Nathan swallowed back a retort. Even his own sister sometimes thought he was still the reckless, irresponsible sibling. "I'll let you know if I need anything, ok?"

"Thanks, Nathan. Listen, don't forget Sunday dinner this week is at my and Dave's place."

"Right," Nathan said. "I'll be sure to look up a really good joke for the girls."

"They loved that one you told them last time about the ducks."

Nathan chuckled. "I'm glad. See you then."

LATE WEDNESDAY MORNING sunlight spilled through the faded lace curtains of the six-by-six window in Dr. O'Neil's study. Ruby was dressed in denim shorts and a lavender-colored cotton T-shirt, with her hair pulled into a ponytail. She stood in the doorway. The patch of light pooled onto the hardwood floor.

She glanced at her phone. Nothing from her advisor in the last 24 hours. She sighed. Bit her lip. When would she hear if she'd gotten selected for an interview?

Ruby's stomach rumbled and she checked her watch. She had to eat something. Even if that chewed up precious time when she should be going through the mountain of paperwork in Dr. O'Neil's office.

She fought down a flutter of panic. She'd stay up every night she was here, if she had to, in order to catalog all of this. She had to get back by next Thursday like she'd promised Dr. Burton.

Her phone buzzed. She picked it up. Maggie.

"Hey, Ruby! How's it going with the professor's papers?"

Ruby gave a laugh. "Uh, I'm feeling a bit overwhelmed, actually. P.E.I.'s beautiful, just like you said it would be. Remind me again why you left?"

"Sometimes I wonder. But that's a long story, actually. So, what do you think of Dr. O'Neil's son?"

Ruby pulled the phone away from her ear and looked at it with raised eyebrows. "How did you know I met him?"

"I figured you were bound to. That city's only 30,000 people."

Ruby fiddled with the hem of her T-shirt. "He seems..." She sighed. The memory of Nathan's blue eyes that first second she'd seen him flashed through her mind. "I've never seen anyone quite as good-looking as he is. No, that isn't true," she said as she realized it with a jolt. "I've never *experienced* anyone as handsome as Nathan is."

"Really?"

Ruby nodded. "You know me. Luke-warm attraction's normal. Chemistry's just for romance novels. And I'd been truly content to keep it firmly between the pages."

"But now?"

"Now it's...more than just physical attraction." She cocked her head and remembered how something in his eyes spoke of second chances... "It's strange. Like, in a way I felt as if I'd missed him.

No, not missed him... More like, hadn't gotten there in time. That makes no sense, though. In time for what? Because I've only just met him."

"Wow. Sounds intense."

"No." Ruby shook her head. "This is *just* attraction." And that, well, that was easy to dismiss. Because she couldn't let herself be attracted to him. She was leaving in a week. And he did have a reputation, if the stories were true. Of course, there was always some kernel of truth in every fiction.

"Well, I need to run. Sourcing some semi-precious stones right now. But send me a text or two, okay?"

"Sure. Talk soon."

She smiled as she ended the call. Stretched and yawned. Her stomach rumbled again, but there was a leaden feeling in there too. What if she couldn't get all of this wrapped up this week? Would that affect her status as a candidate for the special collections position? She had to call Dr. Burton and tell her what was going on. But first, she needed to get some lunch.

She got up and grabbed her purse. The floor slanted slightly underfoot and the boards creaked. She grinned. She'd always loved old buildings. But this one hadn't always been condos.

Ruby looked around. She hadn't gotten an opportunity to check out much of the place last night.

According to the plaque on the sidewalk outside, it had originally been a place called Cross Keys Tavern, built in the 1770s. Now if only cataloging Dr. O'Neil's papers would be as easy as that.

She navigated around piles of papers as she made her way toward the study door. But as she passed the window in the dormer behind Dr. O'Neil's desk, a flash of something caught the corner of her eye.

She turned her head. Nothing.

She started to move away from the spot when the sparkle caught her eye again.

She stepped up to the wavy glass. A tiny crack had somehow caught the sunlight, which caused the glass to shed rainbows through the small space.

She peered closer.

No, she realized. It wasn't a crack.

It was multiple sets of...initials? Done in crude etched lines. Her fingers traced the letters. She rubbed the goose bumps that had suddenly sprouted on her arms and dropped her hand from the window.

Ruby walked out of the study and into the living room, with her purse slung over her shoulder. Just then, the doorknob rattled in the entryway and the door swung open.

Nathan stood on the threshold. "I'm on my lunch break and came to see if you wanted, uh, a sandwich?" Ruby felt a blush creep into her cheeks. That was nice of him.

He held up a Subway bag. Ruby took in his blue eyes fringed by dark lashes; his thick black hair—windblown; his tie—askew. She bit her lip and tried to ignore the way her toes curled. And how she felt like she'd just jumped into a Tilt-A-Whirl. "Thank you." She put a hand to her stomach.

"You okay?" Nathan put one hand on her elbow. With the other, he put the bag of food on a side table.

"Yes," she managed after a moment. She mentally shook her head. He couldn't be affecting her like this.

She felt the warmth of Nathan's fingers seep into her skin.

But she jumped when she realized his thumb had begun to stroke the thin skin on the inside of her elbow.

"Oh, uh, I'm sorry." He dropped his

hand and shoved it into his pocket. Rubbed the back of his neck with his other hand. "You know, I don't normally do that, but you probably wouldn't believe me if I said it, seeing as how...I was doing it."

He trailed off. "Now I'm just making this more awkward." His gaze darted around the room, and his tone became more formal. Distant. "I brought in the last of the boxes. Where would you like me to put them?"

Ruby glanced over her shoulder and followed his line of sight. Five battered banker boxes were neatly stacked in the hallway, a Subway cup tray balanced on the very top box.

Nathan picked up the boxes.

"Nathan, there's—"

But the Subway cup tray had already wobbled and tumbled to the floor, sending a flood of Nestlé Iced Tea and Mountain Dew all over the box and the floor.

"Damn it."

"Here," Ruby said, as she crouched down beside him and picked up the now-soaked top box. "Maybe we can salvage some of it." She placed the wet file on the floor and began to take out all the papers. "You're right," she said, "your dad really was disorganized. Oh." She paused, a receipt she held, poised mid-air between the file and the floor. "I didn't mean—I'm sorry."

"'S'ok," Nathan said, as he continued to mop up the puddle.

Ruby continued to pull out random bits of paper.

Tattered, crumpled electric bills. Out-dated reminder postcards from dentists. Clippings from out-of-print academic journals. Torn, oil-stained gas receipts from 1975. A crumbling, handwritten bill of exchange for a compass.

She'd emptied almost everything from the box and placed it in neat piles on the floor by size and shape.

She peered into the bottom of the box. A red spiral bound notebook, its cover warped by coffee stains, lay in the bottom. She pulled the cheap notebook out and it fell open to the last page filled with cramped yet meticulous handwriting:

"According to an article about Phillips Callbeck in 'The Story of Old Abegweit,' published in 1932, mention is made of a £1000 reward still being in effect for the return of the Great Seal of Prince Edward Island.

I have long speculated as to why

this is the case. Academics believe that the Americans melted it down for bullets, hacked it into pieces for coins, or both.

I have begun developing a theory. What if the American privateer captains came to Charlottetown, raided the city and made off with the seal for another reason than the one presented by history? What if they were on the hunt for a treasure?

I'm still gathering evidence and I can't say for certain what that treasure may be."

"What's that?"

She handed him the notebook and their fingers brushed. Again, that sense of regret edged into her awareness. Huh? She shook it off.

Nathan scanned the writing. "Just another one of his unscientifically supported ideas."

Ruby readjusted her ponytail and stood. She put her hands on her hips. "Why is it that you think your dad was so crazy, exactly? It's not like this is hurting anyone or anything. He was trying to figure something out, here."

Nathan's blue eyes bored into hers. She

wasn't going to be the one to look away first. Nathan crossed his arms. "You want the truth? He was wasting his time. It's just a legend. It's not real facts. Sure, there might've been some truth to it, buried deep, but...come on. Be realistic. Logical. Just because there's some letter that happens to name this woman Edwina, doesn't mean she was some sort of spy for George Washington and had something to do with the Great Seal being stolen. Not to mention that whole speculation about treasure he had. I mean, that sounds like something out of a novel, not real life."

Nathan began to pace. "And now you're here, asking these same questions that my dad did, and—" Nathan sighed and raked a hand through his hair. A flicker of what looked like worry, mixed with anger, flashed across his expression. "I just hate to see anyone waste their life on something that isn't anything more than...than...a colorful island legend."

"Well, I appreciate your..." Ruby narrowed her eyes and shoved her glasses up her nose as she watched Nathan's pace increase, "...concern, but what some people view as 'a colorful island legend,' others have spent years researching and categorizing. It's a part of history, legend or not.

Someone had to write the letter. Someone had to be inspired, had to have that kernel of an idea. And someone had to have heard something that gave them the reason to write it all down."

"Yes, that's all fine and good, but it doesn't mean that every fictional piece of literature is based in fact!" Nathan clenched his hands into fists.

"I know the difference between fairy tales and facts, you know." Ruby tapped her foot.

Nathan had shoved his hands into the back pockets of his charcoal-colored dress pants and turned away to stare out the window.

Ruby couldn't help but admire the fit of those tailored pants—she frowned—even if the man wasn't talking sense.

Nathan turned away from the window to look at her again. "*Do* you?" He rubbed a hand across his stubble. Swallowed. "My dad put all his attention on his research and none on his family. He got so carried away that he forgot about everything else. And I had to pick up the slack."

Ruby watched the sadness, anger and finally resignation, flash across Nathan's face. All at once, she wanted to wrap her arms around him and never let go. To bury her fingers in his hair and nestle against him, to keep him safe and warm.

Her breath quickened. Where it didn't matter what anyone else thought of them or who they were, or where they came from. A surge of righteous indignation washed through her.

No one was going to stand in their way. Not if she could help it.

Ruby mentally shook herself and tapped a finger against her chin instead. Forced aside the strange thoughts. "What're all those letters doing on the window?"

Nathan uncrossed his arms and cocked his head. "What?"

"I'll show you."

Just then, Nathan's cell phone buzzed. He glanced at it and frowned. "It's Evie. She never calls this time of day. I have to take this."

He held his phone up to his ear. Listened. Nodded. "Okay, Evie. I'll come right away." He turned back to Ruby. "Listen uh, hold that thought, will you? I have to get to a meeting with my lawyer."

NATHAN ADJUSTED HIS too-tight tie. He

hunched his shoulders. The last time he'd worn this suit, he'd been practically married.

And look how that had turned out.

But the small leather-bound notebook he'd found at the fort reassured him, somehow. Which is why he'd tucked it, on impulse, into the inside pocket of his suit jacket that he'd thrown on last-minute before he'd headed over here.

Nathan stretched out his long legs in the solicitor's office and glanced over at his sister in the chair next to his.

Evie didn't look too much happier about this. His heart clenched at the sight of his sister. Her short curly brown hair hung rather limply against her forehead. She fiddled with the paperclip that attached all the pages of the hearing documentation together.

"Can anything be done?" Nathan said to his father's long-time friend and attorney.

"My answer, Nathan, is the same as the last time you asked that question," the lawyer answered, her hair cut into a sleek steel-gray bob. "Now, we both know he was a little...eccentric in his ideas, especially in academia. But I don't want to live the rest of my life knowing that I didn't do my duty for him and his family."

She held up her hands. "As you know, his work was very important to him. As was his reputation. And so," the older woman shook her head, "this unfortunate business at the university has threatened everything your father has worked so hard for."

But instead of the paperwork the lawyer was talking about, Nathan found himself thinking about how his pencil had flown across the page so effortlessly. How he'd gotten to that point of euphoric joy as he'd focused completely on the sketch that had seemed to almost draw itself, there on the cliff-top.

He rubbed the back of his neck. The graphic design job definitely didn't do that for him.

Nathan chewed on his lip. Why was this happening now? He'd been perfectly content before this whole thing with his father's research had come to light...

He frowned. Remembered how his dad had appeared to be a caring father but really, he'd only wanted more time to work on yet another research project for his precious tenured position.

Nathan's hands clenched into fists. Dad had always cared more about history and long-dead people than his own family.

Nathan swallowed. Than his own son. Maybe that was a little unfair to judge him so harshly. But Dad's actions hurt.

The lawyer pushed up her horn-rimmed glasses and continued. "UPEI's Board of Governors has come to me."

Nathan shifted in his seat. "Go on."

The lawyer nodded and pushed up her glasses again. "You see," she moved the papers in front of her on the table, "this letter," she held one up for Nathan and he could see the official UPEI letterhead, "accuses your father of falsifying and forging documents."

Nathan frowned. "What the hell is that supposed to mean?"

The lawyer cleared her throat. "I quote one of his colleagues: 'Dr. Gordon O'Neil has severely erred in judgment. Not just once, but multiple times in his career. He should never have received the honor of emeritus, nor should he even be a professor at this institute of higher learning.'" She shuffled her papers. Picked up another one. "This is from another colleague: 'Dr. O'Neil's research is not about legitimate history.' And another: 'O'Neil is wrecking the historical and cultural heritage of the island.'" She met Nathan's gaze. "These are all previous claims. But now, combined with this..." She indicated the official letter and shook her head.

Her glossy bob gleamed in the light from the window behind her. "The thing is," she said, then shrugged and spread her hands wide in a gesture of surrender. "Everyone knew what your father was like. But as time went on, his colleagues began to suspect he was helping himself out to bolster his credibility in the theories he was formulating about the theft of the Great Seal in 1775."

Nathan stared at her. "What?" His jaw clenched.

"These charges claim that your father forged the signed order of General George Washington—dated 23 November, 1775—about Edwina Belliveaux."

"What I don't understand," Nathan said, as he leaned forward in his seat. His eyes flashed, "is why. The O'Neils have always had a stellar reputation on the island here." A muscle in Nathan's jaw ticked. "My father may have been a crackpot," he said between clenched teeth. "But he has never done anything illegal." Nathan crossed his arms.

"I'm sorry, Nathan, but that's why I asked you and your sister into the office here. Because it looks like this is really quite serious. Before your father died, he'd published a paper on his latest findings. It raised the ire of those colleagues of his who I quoted earlier. They claimed he'd forged the order. Now," the lawyer rubbed her temples and took off her glasses, "this could lead to a serious investigation. Against not only the paper he'd published and his claims about the seal, but also against his whole life's work."

"So," Evie said, "what are we supposed to do about it?"

"Well," the lawyer said, "you have two options."

Nathan perched on the edge of his seat.

"One," the lawyer raised a hand and ticked off the points on her fingers, "you can ignore it and hope it goes away. Which it won't. Or," she adjusted a strand of her hair, "you can take the governors to court. Sue them for defamation of character, that sort of thing..."

"Or," Nathan said, as he stood and began to pace, "we can disprove these claims." He glanced over at his sister and then at the lawyer. "You both know I hate to fight. But," he ran a hand through his hair. "This isn't right."

He put his palms down on the table. The smooth mahogany surface gleamed.

"Because," he said, as his eyes met the lawyer's, then his sister's, "we all know Dad was an upstanding citizen."

"Exactly," Evie said.

Nathan fiddled with the spare change in his pocket. Began to pace faster. "But if we don't do something, then no one will remember Dad that way. We can fix it." He paused. "We just need to gather the evidence. And show the governors that they don't know what they're talking about." Nathan rubbed the back of his neck and clenched his teeth. Injustice had always bothered him. Wrongs *had* to be righted. Dad was *family*.

Evie cocked her head. "He was working on that research project about the Great Seal."

The lawyer tapped a fingernail against her temple. "Dr. O'Neil told me that he was beginning to realize that the lost seal, if it could be found, may be the key to figuring out Edwina's real role in history. That she was somehow connected to it in ways people hadn't imagined.

"But—" she paused and shuffled some papers, "—we both know how stubborn Islanders are about changing their out-look." The lawyer continued. "The hearing's two weeks from today."

"Well, there's only one thing to do." Nathan put his hands on his hips. "I need to find the original order. It's the only way to clear things up." This had to be made right. His fingers brushed the small leather-bound volume. He couldn't—he wouldn't—let those in power take away what wasn't rightfully theirs. He gripped the book. Not from someone he loved. Not this time. Not again. He looked down and discovered he had clutched the small leather-bound book so hard his knuckles had turned white. *Not again*? He frowned. Where had that thought come from?

His mind strayed back to Ruby. Wait. He could ask her...for help? He could ask her what she thought they could do about it, anyway.

She'd found that letter fragment, after all. And she believed Dad. She had a copy of the order he'd sent her...

It'd be a place to start, anyway.

"It's the only way to clear Dad's name. So I'd better get started."

There was no way he was going to let his father's good name be dragged through the mud. He had to set things right. And if that meant working with Ruby, figuring out if there really was something behind all this, well, so be it.

RUBY LOOKED AROUND at the vast piles of paperwork on the floor next to the desk. Now that she'd made a bit of a dent, and organized the late professor's desk, she realized she needed some sort of filing system for these piles on the floor.

She tapped a forefinger against her chin. Snuck a look at her phone. Still nothing from her advisor. She sighed. Best to focus on her work and put that out of her mind for now.

Well, in reverse order by date was always a good place to start. She rifled through the pages of her legal pad until she found a clean sheet. Then she began to write dates in back-slanting, block letters and made sure to leave space between each entry.

The easy part was over.

Ruby reached for the nearest box, the one that looked the messiest. She pried the lid off and peered in. A moldy half-eaten gingerbread cookie lay inside.

She hadn't thought to bring rubber gloves.

Using a spare piece of paper, she reached in, picked up the cookie and threw it into the trash. Underneath the grease stains was a series of pages bound together with rubber bands. Photocopies, from the looks of it.

She flipped through them. They all seemed to be talking about the same thing. A reference to that thousand-pound reward. From an article in *The Island* magazine dated... Ruby pushed her glasses up her nose and squinted at the almost-indecipherable scribble in the margin...2 May, 1875.

She withheld a sigh. So far, nothing had come to light having to do with the love letter fragment or just who Edwina had received the letter from. Not that she should be surprised. Dr. O'Neil had said he didn't have the other half. Maybe she'd come all the way up here for nothing.

Ruby glanced at the time on her phone. Nathan's meeting with the lawyer was taking awhile. Was it about Dr. O'Neil? Or something else entirely? She shrugged. It wasn't really any of her business.

And it didn't really matter, except that he said he'd help her sort through more of the boxes. Which was nice of him. Not that she needed any help. She'd devised her own particular filing system so that—

A short knock on the door to the condo

interrupted her thoughts. A second later, she heard the door open and then shut.

She glanced over her shoulder. Nathan had come back.

He walked into the room, and Ruby's heart fluttered. He nodded in her direction as he rubbed a hand across his unshaven jaw. "How's it going?"

"Uh, pretty well," she said, "But now that you're back, can you tell me about those initials in the window?"

"...Uh, sure." He glanced at his phone. Put it back in his pocket. "Where?" She showed Nathan the spot she'd been standing in earlier.

He reached a fingertip up to trace the tiny series of letters. "Been there as long as I can remember." He cocked his head. "I think it started back when the tavern was built. Couples would etch their initials in the glass when they got engaged."

He leaned against the window ledge behind his father's desk. The window, Ruby noticed, looked like it was original to the 1700s. She smiled. "Well, that's certainly romantic."

"Yeah. It's a bit of a tourist draw, actually. Dad would never let anyone up here, but it's been mentioned on the walking tours around downtown."

Nathan rubbed a finger along a heart carved into the window ledge. "This has been here for ages too."

"Really?" Ruby peered over his shoulder. "That's so neat."

Nathan's lips curved up. "Yeah, I guess it is. Funny how you don't think much about things you've seen all your life. Like this study." He paused. Looked around. "I remember Dad would make me stay up here for hours when I was in high school. On hot August days like this. When I'd rather be bridge-jumping along Covehead Road with my buddies."

Ruby's eyes widened.

"You jump off at a certain angle so you don't knock yourself out, and the bridges aren't that high from the water." Nathan grinned and raised his eyebrows. "Everyone did it. The cold Gulf of St. Lawrence feels great when it's hot out. Much more fun than sorting through dusty documents." He raised a palm. "No offense to present company."

Ruby laughed. "Back in high school—and even now—I'd *rather* sort through dusty documents or read at the library than do crazy things like that. Libraries have air conditioning." She shot him a grin. "Though I do like going to the beach.

Especially at sunset. Walking barefoot through the surf..." She leaned back against the desk. "Although the New England coastline isn't anything like the shorelines up here. At least, from the photos I saw and the view out the airplane window. It's all sandy beaches and high dunes."

"Along the north shore, yep." Nathan nodded. "That's something I don't take for granted. The natural beauty around here."

Ruby sighed. "It's so gorgeous." She straightened up. "So. How was the meeting with the lawyer?"

Nathan sighed. He rested both palms on the wooden window ledge, which creaked with the weight. Ruby couldn't help but notice the line of muscle on his arms flex as he did so. She cleared her throat.

"Not so good. My dad's been accused of forging documents." His hands tightened into fists. He leaned back further, and eased his full weight onto the ledge. "So I'd like to help you find that November 23 order of Washington's. It's the only way I can clear Dad's name. Prove he wasn't forging it. He might've been a crackpot, but he wasn't a criminal." Nathan compressed his lips then glanced at Ruby.

"Oh." Ruby's mouth suddenly went dry

and she rubbed her palms on her jeans. Nathan? Here? In her space? How was she supposed to think, with him around all the time? She had a method. A strategy. He wasn't an academic.

She glanced at him and tucked a strand of hair behind her ear then wet her lips. No. No. Be a professional. She'd just think of him as her...assistant. Right. That would work. He was asking for her help. She could give it. "Okay," she said at last.

Nathan's shoulders relaxed. He met her gaze. "Thank you," he said.

"You're welcome." She pushed up her glasses.

"I appreciate your...giving me a chance. Some credit." His smile was lopsided. "Dad never did."

Ruby just nodded. "Well, he said he found it originally in a psalm book. So maybe if we look there first..."

"Okay. Whatever you think."

Ruby brought a hand up and absently played with the locket around her neck. Having Nathan around felt like the right thing to do. The right choice.

"That's pretty. Where did you get it?" Nathan nodded in her direction.

"What? Oh—" She glanced at the lock-et. "A flea market a couple years ago in

Boston's North End. Got a great deal."

"Deals are always good."

"Yep. Turns out, when I had it appraised, it was made in the 1700s. The jeweller thought it looked like Paul Revere's work. I just like it for the sentimental value. Though the possible historical aspect is pretty neat too, I thought." She flicked open the locket. "See? The two pictures?"

Nathan took a step closer. "Those have great detail in them. That's amazing."

"Yeah. In fact, I found something underneath the man's portrait just the other day. Some sort of rhyme or puzzle or something."

"Really? I love puzzles and stuff like that. Can I see it?"

She rummaged around in her pocket. "Here."

Cardinal directions of the heart
Impart the way toward True North
Good-hearted General's Orders did put forth;
Crowned Head of Justice, strong and brave
Cradled on the wind and waves

Nathan bent his head to examine the slip of paper. Ruby couldn't help but notice the way the afternoon light glinted off his black hair.

"The whole thing sounds like some sort of..."—he laughed—"...riddle."

"That's what I said when I first saw it."

"Cradled on the wind and waves..." Nathan murmured to himself.

"Do you know what that means?"

"I'm not sure. But I do know that the Mi'kmaq people called Prince Edward Island *abegweit,* which means, basically, 'cradled on the waves.'"

Ruby's eyes widened.

"Look." Nathan pointed to the phrase. *"Good-hearted General's Orders.* It's capitalized..." Nathan began to pace. "Orders. General..." He held up his hands. "Of course. Washington was a general during the war, right?"

Ruby slowly nodded.

"Didn't you say he had those two orders? It's more than coincidence. One of which refers to the seal. And the other refers to...

"...P.E.I., maybe?" Ruby flipped to a clean page on her legal pad.

"Yes," Nathan said, "that's it. So crowned head would be referring to, well, someone in authority."

"Crowned...that means royal." Ruby commented, as she began to affix paperclips to the neat piles of papers she'd stacked on the professor's desk. "Royal. Like, a queen."

"Or king." Nathan ruffled his hair. "King George III. That *could* to be a reference to the seal."

Ruby slipped the unused paperclips into their paper container. "So King George III...what about the justice part?"

"He commissioned the seal, and the seal is what makes legal documents official. So, justice refers to that. It only makes logical sense." Nathan grinned.

Ruby nodded. "...Right. Yes. That does." She cocked her head and held his gaze for a moment.

"But what about cardinal directions of the heart?" She bit her lip. "That phrase sounds so familiar...but why? Of the heart..." she murmured and tucked a strand of hair behind her ear. "Cardinal directions..." Her eyes widened. "Of course. It's that same phrase as in the letter fragment. Well, not exactly the same. But similar. That means this could have something to do with a compass."

"And true north," Nathan added, "that's a direction on a compass. The compass pointing toward north."

"Yes, but true north. Capitalized."

Nathan shifted. "Well, there *is* an island legend about a compass that's supposed to point toward your true love, instead of true north. So I think you're right—it's definitely referring to a compass."

"Wow."

"Yeah. And speaking of lovers, it's speculated that Molly McDuff, the first postmistress in Charlottetown, wrote a poem called *The Fair Isle Lovers*. It's thought she was writing about someone she knew. But that hasn't been proven. She lived and worked here in the tavern all her life. That's what these condos used to be. Up here was the storage area for the tavern. They probably kept barrels of rum and salt pork and things like that up here. Anyway, Molly was sort of the unofficial postmistress at the time, too. Over the years, people have discovered the occasional postcard or letter lying around this building."

"You know quite a bit."

Nathan shifted beside her. "Yeah, well, listening to Dad all the time, I guess I picked up a few things."

She leaned forward and her eyes lingered on his mouth. She tore her gaze away. No. She was being ridiculous. How could she feel so attracted to him? She was leaving next week. Besides, they lived in different countries.

Not only that, she had a job to do. She had to be professional. She was just here to finish cataloging these papers.

She didn't have time to get involved with some local. Especially not this local. The conversation between those two older women ran through her mind again.

Not only that, she'd read enough romance novels to know that bad boys on the page and bad boys in real life were two different things.

Nathan raked a hand through his hair. "That poem's just a bunch of romantic nonsense. Made up before there was TV or the internet to entertain people." He shook his head. "When will people see sense?"

"Speaking of seeing sense—what about this?" She pointed at the page again. "This means..."

Nathan looked down at the page too. "Well, based on what we've figured out...this riddle is talking about the lost Great Seal of Prince Edward Island. This could help clear Dad's name."

Ruby frowned. "But we're already trying to find that order. And I have all these papers to catalog. We don't have time for this."

ALONE IN HIS house that evening, Nathan tugged at the hem of his white cotton T-shirt and then pulled it over his head. The movement made his hair ruffle as he tossed the shirt in the general direction of the laundry hamper.

Then he unzipped the fly of his dark-wash, slightly faded jeans. He shucked them off too, which left him in just his Calvin Kleins.

God, he couldn't stop thinking about her. Ruby. He shook his head.

No. He needed to get back to his sketchpad. That's what he really needed to do. It was the only thing that kept him centered these days.

But somehow, that seascape he'd so eagerly sketched had fizzled and lay in uninspired flatness in his mind.

The way the light had reflected Ruby's glossy waves, and the gold flecks in the hazel depths of her eyes—His fingers twitched.

He had to draw her.

Huh?

He'd never attempted a portrait before. But...that would get her out of his thoughts and onto the paper. Then maybe he could concentrate on his work again. Keep making progress with his new site design for Parks Canada's offices on P.E.I.

He couldn't imagine living anywhere else than this island. Just look at it. The sand dunes. The seagulls. The feel of the sun on his skin. Why would anyone want to go anywhere else? It had everything he needed. But perhaps not everything he wanted...

Nathan ruffled his hair even further. As he jammed a hand through it, he ambled into the master ensuite bathroom and squeezed toothpaste onto his brush.

Nathan's mind wandered to the way Ruby had looked at him behind her brown tortoiseshell glasses. He couldn't suppress the way his gut wrenched.

God. Those big hazel eyes... Full of intelligence. Spirit. He grinned. He liked that about her. And she was smart. Smarter than he'd ever be. Going for her doctorate. Wow. But that was okay. He liked smart women.

He leaned against the sink.

What the hell was going on? Nathan spit out the toothpaste and turned on the tap.

He shook his head. She wasn't an Islander. She was American, besides all that. What's more, she would be gone soon. Out of his life.

He didn't need to complicate things by adding the disappointment of yet another failed relationship to his list.

He swallowed.

Just like all the ones before.

But this hollow space in his heart had somehow grown in the last few days and he wished he had someone to at least...talk to.

He let the tap run for a second then he leaned forward and splashed cold water on his face. The cool droplets brought back a sense of centeredness. Normalcy.

He took a breath and reached across the mirrored medicine cabinet to grab a towel. He began to dry his face when an image rose in his mind's eye.

He froze. Then yanked open the bathroom vanity drawer and fished out the small sketchpad and pencil he kept there for times like this when inspiration struck.

In one swift movement, he flipped the pad to a clean sheet and put pencil to paper.

He could see her in his mind's eye, as if through an out of focus camera lens. A woman's face. A beautiful face. A haunted face. He began to sketch in long, fluid strokes.

His breath quickened.

Bringing her to life.

A shiver ran through him.

He watched his pencil move across the paper. Watched, as if looking at someone else's hand, not his own, began to shade in details.

Her cheeks, streaked with dirt and tears. Though her eyes were hidden by the brim of a battered tricorn hat, he could almost *feel* her features: taunt with anger and hope. And her handkerchief torn and speckled with...was that blood?

Nathan swallowed down the sudden lump in his throat, as he now felt that same surge of longing and regret he'd experienced in the hallway.

His head began to pound as if he had a migraine. His heart throbbed and ached, like he had just lost his best friend and his only true love. As Nathan continued to sketch the picture in his head, he saw, in his mind's eye, the woman's lips move.

His pencil moved even faster across the page as he raced to capture the curve of her lips, the hint of a tender smile underneath all that sadness.

She brought a crumpled piece of paper

up to her heart. Her hand clenched into a fist as she did.

He shook his head and clenched his jaw. But kept sketching.

At last, he stopped. A bead of sweat trickled down between his shoulder blades. The blood pounded in his veins.

He stared down at the page. He'd done it. She was absolutely beautiful. How was this possible? He'd never drawn anything like this in his life. He'd never even drawn people before. Only landscapes.

And even those looked nothing like this. Nothing this...good. This lifelike. It wasn't logical.

Because this...this wasn't a picture of Ruby, as he'd intended to draw. This was a picture of a woman from the 1700s. He swallowed. Dug his nails into his palms. What if logic couldn't explain what had just happened?

Chapter Four

THURSDAY MORNING, RUBY'S cell phone buzzed. She glanced at the caller ID. Dr. Burton.

"Ruby, how's it going?"

"I was going to call you in a little while because I have some, uh, news." Ruby bit her lip. "Dr. Gordon O'Neil's papers are a bit more...messy than I thought. This could take awhile. But," she hurried on, "I'll be back to prep for my defense."

As Ruby opened her mouth to explain more, her advisor said, "Actually that's not why I called. Have you checked your email?"

"I, uh, haven't had a chance to yet."

"Well, congratulations! You got selected for the job interview."

Ruby sank onto the wingback chair. Her heart hammered. "But this cataloging may end up taking two weeks. Maybe even more..." And now that they had the riddle situation? She'd realized Nathan had been right—it could help clear his dad's name, and just might help with her love letter research, too. "When is the interview scheduled for?"

"9 a.m. Monday."

"In four days?"

"This hiring committee likes to move things along."

Ruby shifted the phone to her other ear.

"If you get this position, Ruby, it could really make your career. It's tenure-track."

Ruby's stomach clenched. "But I think there's more here than I originally thought."

Dr. Burton gave a shaky laugh. Then sighed. Ruby could almost see her rub her forehead.

Ruby felt a bead of sweat form between her shoulder blades. She couldn't lose Nathan—couldn't *leave* him. Right. That's what she meant.

She'd come too far to back out now. The only way to find out more would be to take the time to go through things. Study the documents. And help Nathan find the order. "I can't leave yet. I'm uncovering things that might be very valuable for my dissertation defense. But I also want to be considered for the job."

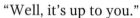

"Well, it's up to you."

Ruby let out the breath she'd held. "I'll do as much as I can here now, then go back for the interview, and see what happens."

For a second, Dr. Burton didn't say anything. Then, she spoke. "You know, Ruby, we've spent so much time together in the department that it practically feels like you're family. So if you need anything, don't hesitate to let me know."

"Thanks." Ruby smiled. "I'll do that."

She hit end and slid the phone back into her purse. She stared up at the cracked ceiling, and blinked rapidly.

Family.

She bit her lip. She'd never known hers. Not her biological one, anyway.

And, if she was honest with herself, that's why she'd become an academic to begin with. She'd felt like maybe one day, if she dug deep enough, far enough, back into someone else's past, she'd find her own.

What was she going to do now that everything had changed? No, she shook her head. She knew exactly what she was going to do. She was going to do what she always did when faced with a challenge.

Get to the bottom of things. She grinned. Yet another reason she loved history and academics. It gave her persistence.

She picked up her pen and notepad and began to jot notes.

AFTER WORK THURSDAY, in his basement spare room, Nathan studied the sketch of the woman in the tricorn hat that he'd now transposed onto the canvas.

His brow furrowed. How did he know how to do all this? He knew more about computers and the latest graphic design program than his way around a boar-bristle paintbrush.

Yet he dipped the brush into the cerulean on the palette he held in his other hand, and brought it to the canvas.

But he paused. The blood pounded in his temples. His fingertips tingled and his heart—almost in his throat.

A low chuckle escaped him. Could he do this with his eyes closed?

On impulse, he did just that.

All at once, the woman's face came back to him; this time clearer, sharper, and more in focus.

Without thinking, he lifted the paintbrush to the canvas. The bristles touched the surface.

And this strange pent-up yearning, longing, and disappointment poured through him. All at once, his brush began to move.

The exact shade of her green eyes: sea foam flicked with bottle-green and emerald.

The way that her hair caught the candlelight and reflected a million little diamond points of light.

The low, soft way she laughed. The rustle of the pale pink silk of her skirts. The crackle of the flames in the grate as he mixed color after color, a frown of concentration between his brows. The scent of wood smoke and pine mixed with the sharp tang of iron-gall ink and the fuller, heavy-bodied scent of oil paints.

Every muscle in his body tightened, strained, as his brush flew across the canvas. Nathan felt his breathing shift: light yet deep. The long, sure strokes of his brush moved almost too fast to be discernible.

Yet still he painted.

He became aware of only the next color, the next shade, the next piece of the puzzle that would finally fit together everything into one complete whole, into one moment, one second, one suspended transcendent place in time where she was his and he was hers and everything was right.

His chest heaved. His heart swelled. His throat tightened and his jaw clenched.

He gasped for breath even as his eyes flew open.

Nathan's jagged breaths finally settled and evened out as he forced himself to stop and look at what he'd done.

He felt strands of his hair stick to his forehead; he wiped a forearm across it. A broad grin spread across his face. He wiped his fingers on the paint-stained rag before tucking it into the back pocket of his ripped and faded jeans now splattered with paint. He'd done it. He'd actually painted a portrait.

He couldn't stop staring.

*There she was. Whole and beautiful and completely his. To have and to hold til death doth part—A heavy leaden weight filled his heart at the sight of her green eyes. No. Anger flickered. She'd let him down. And he hadn't made it to her in time. He reached out, the satiny smoothness of her cheek under his fingertips as he—*Nathan flinched. He'd never seen this woman before in his life. He gazed at her features. Wait a minute...

He sucked in a breath. Yes. Yes he had.

It was Edwina Belliveaux. Why had he painted *her*?

His hands started to tremble. He had no idea about her personal life, who she was, who she loved. Or why he'd given her the vivid hazel of Ruby's eyes.

Damn it. His hands shook and he fisted them into his hair.

Nothing about this made any logical sense. Especially when he saw that he'd painted her holding a red-and-white rosebud.

FRIDAY MORNING, RUBY stifled a yawn and blinked sleep out of her eyes. She'd been up far too late last night thinking about—

"Ready to get started on the hunt for Washington's order this morning?" Nathan said as he walked into the room. "I was able to get the day off work today."

"Oh, um, that's great," Ruby jumped, and a blush crept across her cheeks. She smoothed out an imaginary wrinkle from the sleeveless fuchsia polka-dot sundress she wore. Thank goodness he hadn't been able to read her thoughts. Especially since they had, unfortunately, involved him.

He wore a cobalt-blue T-shirt and a pair of faded jeans. His hair was slightly damp from a shower. He smelled like cinnamon and pine needles, Ruby noticed, as he came to stand beside her on the Aubusson rug in the middle of Dr. O'Neil's study.

But after a couple hours, the only thing they'd discovered were out-dated bank statements, a handful of newspaper clippings about colleagues' accomplishments, and copies of Dr. O'Neil's 4000-level course syllabi from last year.

Nathan stood and stretched. Glanced at the grandfather clock against the far wall as it gonged 11 a.m. "Ready for an early lunch?"

Ruby nodded. "We can meet back here in forty-five minutes."

"Oh," Nathan shoved his hands into his pockets, "I meant, maybe we could get some lunch together."

Ruby bit her lip. Looked away from his direct gaze. She'd be gone in a few days.

"Don't worry, I won't bite. I thought we could talk about the riddle and where it might lead next," he added.

She *did* need to eat. "Well," Ruby pushed up her glasses. "All right." Her grip on her legal pad relaxed. "But I'm paying."

Nathan made a sweeping gesture with his hand toward the door. "Of course. After you."

After they grabbed menus at the coffee shop called Kettle Black across the street and placed their orders, they found seats at a table outside. Nathan turned to Ruby. "So. The riddle."

But before Ruby could answer, she heard, "Nathan! How *are* you?" Ruby glanced over her shoulder. A young woman with long curly red hair walked up to the outdoor seating area a few feet from their table. She carried a blue paper shopping bag, and the bright yellow cotton of her sundress fluttered in the breeze.

Ruby saw Nathan shift in his seat. "Zoe. Uh, hi. I'm good. You?" He swallowed. Darted his gaze to Ruby.

"Great," the woman replied. "I haven't seen you in ages."

Nathan tugged at his earlobe. "Uh, yeah. Been awhile."

The red-haired woman laughed. "Listen, I just wanted to say I'm glad it didn't work out between us. Because," she flashed her left hand, "I'm now engaged." She grinned. "So thank you."

Nathan hunched his shoulders. "Um, sure." Rattled the ice in his glass.

The red-haired woman smiled. "Looks like that's all water under the bridge now, anyway." She glanced at Ruby then back to Nathan. "Oh!" She looked at her watch. "Gotta run. Take care, Nathan. Nice to see you again."

Nathan fiddled with the straw in his water glass. "You too, Zoe. And congratulations."

So that was one of Nathan's exes...Or, Ruby's stomach clenched, one of his ex-*fiancées*? She bit her lip. No, it didn't matter.

"You were right." Ruby blurted out.

"I was?"

"This riddle." She twisted a strand of hair around her ponytail. Met Nathan's gaze. "It really got me to thinking." Their food arrived.

"Did it?" Nathan said, after he swallowed a bite of his crab salad.

"There is..." she traced a fingertip along the edge of her plate, "something there."

"So," Nathan leaned forward, "what do you think the next thing to look for is?"

"I don't know. Besides the seal, I mean. Which we don't have."

Nathan frowned.

Ruby sighed.

Nathan shook his head and sat back in

his chair.

"Sometimes historical things are like that," she said softly. "You think you'll find something great and it turns out to be nothing. Or only leads to more questions." Ruby took another bite of her battered cod and realized Nathan was watching her. She felt heat surge through her, but forced herself to concentrate on her meal.

"So." Nathan cocked his head and studied her. "Do you have any brothers or sisters?"

"I'm an only child."

"I have an older sister, as you already know." He paused. "That must have been nice having no one to argue with, growing up."

"Not really. I was...adopted. I never knew my real parents." She paused. Fiddled with her napkin. "I don't actually know if I have any siblings." Ruby looked up and met his gaze. Something about the openness of his expression tugged at her and she found herself continue. "I used to have this...recurring daydream, I guess you could call it, starting when I was four or five." She cleared her throat. Glanced at him. He nodded encouragement.

She'd never told anyone this before yet she wanted, suddenly, to tell him every last detail of it. "I would imagine myself sitting on a wooden bench in a tiny stone house, with a huge fire blazing in the hearth, my brothers and sister beside me. Our parents were there, too. I felt..." She lowered her voice. "So safe and warm."

Her gaze darted to, then away from Nathan's. "Like I belonged." She fiddled with her napkin. "I loved that daydream. I'd play it over and over again in my head whenever I was angry at my adoptive parents. Or had a bad day at school."

"Wow, that's pretty specific for a day-dream." Nathan leaned forward.

"Yeah, I always thought so too. Made me wonder if maybe it was a past-life memory or something." She ate another fork-full of her battered cod. Then asked, "What about your parents?"

"My mom died when I was seventeen. Hit by a drunk driver when she was coming home from one of my school plays. It was the middle of January. Haven't liked winter since."

"Oh, I'm so sorry."

"Thanks."

Ruby opened her mouth to ask Nathan another question but heard someone calling Nathan's name behind her again.

"Oh, hi there, Nathan."

Ruby took the last few bites of her lunch and looked up in time to see another young woman—a petite blonde—walk by. She waved in Nathan's direction.

Ruby watched Nathan give the blonde woman a quick smile and wave back even while his gaze shifted to Ruby's. He cleared his throat then fiddled with his silverware.

Was that the most recent woman he'd rejected? Maybe there was some truth to what those ladies had said... How many women *had* Nathan dated, anyway?

Ruby wiped her lips with her napkin. Well, really, it shouldn't matter. "Ready to head back?" She pulled out her debit card and, after she paid, quickly checked her account balance. Only $500 left in her savings account. How had that happened? Her student loan payment might have to be deferred this month, too. She worried her bottom lip between her teeth.

Nathan nodded. "Let's go."

They crossed Queen Street and headed up to the condo again.

Ruby picked up the next cardboard box and took off the lid. More jumbled papers. She bit back a groan and started to riffle through them.

Underneath a stack of photocopies was a cloth-bound book. Its corners had frayed and its spine had cracked. The title, *From Away*, in gold leaf, had mostly flaked off. Ruby picked it up as if she held a newborn kitten.

"What's fascinating you so much there?" Nathan's voice was far too close to her ear. She jumped and spun around in the red leather chair behind Dr. O'Neil's desk.

She hastily set the book down. She hoped he hadn't noticed its back cover had nearly fallen off, thanks to her jerky motion.

Nathan raised his eyebrows. "That looks like one of my father's."

Ruby looked down at the book and traced a finger across its surface.

Nathan frowned. "Don't worry about the back cover. These things are old."

"Right. So," Ruby bent forward and nudged a discarded accordion file with her sandaled toe, then picked it up and threw it in the wastebasket. "I've been doing some cleaning up."

"I can see that," Nathan said, and leaned against the desk top next to the large red leather chair.

She opened the book. Mustiness wafted to her. The flyleaf was warped and the title page was torn in half. She discovered that most of the pages were glued together with age and damp.

But a list of names near the back of the book, in a neatly typed column, caught her eye. It listed all the people who had immigrated to Prince Edward Island before 1800. Half the names were Scottish. The rest, from the looks of it, were Irish, with a smattering of French settlers, too. Acadians, she realized. Belliveaux was listed. Edwina's people?

She had lowered the book halfway to the desktop when the back cover fell completely off. Ruby reached out to pick it up, a hand to her mouth.

But that's when she noticed that the end paper had come loose. And just visible where the end paper and the board of the back cover met, was the edge of a second piece of paper.

Ruby's forehead creased as she used her thumb and forefinger to pull the page free.

She sighed in relief. They'd found it. The signed order from General Washington. Now Dr. O'Neil's name could be cleared.

But wait. She unfolded and skimmed the document. This wasn't an order. It was a letter...

"Nathan," she whispered as she carefully smoothed out the page. "Look at this."

He began to read over her shoulder, aloud. His breath caressed her cheek:

—and how my heart longs but for the taste of your kiss, the feel of your arms around me. Perhaps it goes against propriety to speak of such things so boldly, yet this missive is for your eyes alone.

Nathan's voice was low, soft, deep, in her ear. Ruby felt a thrill go up her spine.

Darling, I did not expect, though I should have guessed, I would be jailed for desertion. On 27 November, only a few days after we arrived in Boston Harbor. But now that I have escaped imprisonment for choosing not to fight in this War, I shall do my damnedest to reach you on St. John's Island. Indeed, I journey there now. But with it being midwinter and with my unfortunate location at present in the midst of these Rebellious Colonies, I fear these events and circumstances do not afford me much hope that I shall reach you in time.

A sense of longing and desire—for what, Ruby couldn't say—coursed through her. Tears sprang to her eyes and she swallowed, as Nathan continued to read.

Oh, how I so much desire to speak on your behalf against the supposed crimes that these unfeeling Monsters seem to think you have engendered! How could Washington fathom you had stolen the Seal for your own ends then send you back to the island?

Nathan's voice had lowered to a whisper, and his breath was warm on her skin.

Thus, I pray this letter be a part of me that shall reach you, give you all the strength, warmth and love you need in order to withstand their cries for blood. I pray it shall not be yours that is spilt.

I am Your most Faithful servant
Alexander

Nathan had stopped speaking. Silence clung to them both, heavy and deep. She didn't want to disturb it, somehow. Didn't want to break the moment, the fragility of whatever-it-was that hung between them, now. Yet her chest felt tight. Hollow. She couldn't leave him. And suddenly, she wanted to turn around, wrap her arms around Nathan, and never let go.

Her heart pounded.

She could feel it, feel all that was unspoken, as it shimmered between them. But it was more than his voice. It was something about the *way* he'd said those words. In that tone. Soft. Low...As if it was a promise. A promise left unfulfilled... Goose bumps broke out on her bare arms and she rubbed them.

"Cold?" Nathan murmured, and placed his warm hands on her exposed skin.

She sucked in a breath as she felt his hands on her. And suddenly, she wanted to stay here, in this moment, with this man, on this island...forever.

Her eyes fluttered closed. Then snapped open.

This island. Washington. The seal. She gasped. "Wait a minute."

Nathan cleared his throat. Dropped his arms from her.

"This is the other half." She spun around. "The other half of the love letter fragment. It was actually *here*. This is huge!"

Nathan crossed his arms and shifted

away from Ruby to lean against the desk. "That's great."

She chewed on a cuticle. "Hmm. But Dr. O'Neil said he didn't *have* the other half." She met Nathan's gaze.

"Well," he said, "it was hidden inside a book. I doubt my dad even knew it was there."

Ruby flushed. "Right." She looked up after she re-read the letter to herself. "This means...Alexander was who Edwina had received the letter from. He didn't want to fight in the war." She rummaged around in her notes and pulled out the copy of the first half of the letter fragment.

"Draft dodger?"

Ruby shook her head. Scanned the lines. "The penalty for desertion was death. But only if you got caught. Look at this."

"Well," Nathan said, after he read the letter in whole. "I remember from this lecture one of my ex-girlfriends dragged me to, something about Quakers coming up here in the 1700s because they were pacifists. So maybe that's why he was going up here to begin with? Maybe that's how he met her?"

"That's possible."

The lines from the other half of the

letter jumped out at her: *the compass of the heart points in new directions.*

Did this mean that first riddle had something to do with this letter? With the order? The seal?

Nathan glanced at her. "Do you think this has to do with the order? And the seal?"

Ruby laughed. "That's just what I was thinking!"

"Great minds." Nathan grinned. "How about we go to the public library to try to find out?"

Ruby just couldn't snuff out the hopeful look in his blue eyes. The public library was the least likely place to find anything related to the in-depth information they needed. But, who knew? It would be at least a place to start.

"All right," she said. "Let's go."

Somehow she couldn't quite bring herself to tell him she was leaving Sunday for an interview. One that might, if she got the job, force her to abandon everything she'd started to help with, here.

RUBY AND NATHAN took a left out of Cross Keys Condos and headed up the slight incline toward Great George Street. Ruby noticed three brightly colored row houses on the opposite side of the street. A bronze statue depicted not one but two men dressed in coattails and top hats. They gestured over a document that lay spread out on a barrel. Ruby smiled. She'd have to come back by here and read the plaque.

It had started to drizzle and Ruby pulled up the hood of her purple zippered sweatshirt. Her hair always seemed to frizz in the humidity. She blew away a strand that had fallen across her eyes.

What happened back there in Dr. O'Neil's study? She felt herself cringe. She'd just been overly hopelessly romantic. Or something. Just...too affected by the words of someone long dead. That was all.

She darted a glance at Nathan. He seemed unaffected by their earlier...incident? Encounter?

The drizzle increased.

Up ahead, she noticed a homeless man. The hood of his white windbreaker was cinched around his face. The Tim Horton's paper coffee cup he held was half-full of coins and water as he hunched in the doorway of a three-story red brick building. Nathan reached into his jeans pocket and tossed a few dollars into the man's cup. "Buy yourself some hot coffee."

Ruby's heart swelled in her chest.

But in the next second, a knot formed in her stomach. Based on what had happened when she and Nathan had had lunch together this afternoon, it seemed those ladies on Victoria Row must have been right...

They continued up the block. Ruby paused to glance up at St. Dunstan's tall spires; its golden limestone almost glowed in the late morning sun.

But someone who gave money to the homeless couldn't be all bad, could he?

They reached Richmond Street. After they crossed the brick-paved pedestrian street, they headed up the steps of the Confederation Center of the Arts with its 1960s facade and two-story high plate-glass windows.

But the thin man with steel-rimmed glasses and salt-and-pepper hair who sat behind the reference desk on the second floor shook his head. "There's nothing about a second signed order from General George Washington."

"Oh no," Nathan said and glanced at Ruby.

The reference librarian looked up from his desk. His steel-rimmed glasses caught the fluorescent lights. "We do have a file on the theft of the Great Seal, though. Everything's in it. Typed copies of the original letters that Wright and Callbeck wrote to the Earl of Dartmouth telling him what happened. A copy of the order from General Washington telling Captains Broughton and Selman not to bother any Canadian ships. Even a copy of a pencil sketch some travelling diplomat did of the original Great Silver Seal, as it's sometimes called. The one you're looking for. Er," he chuckled, "I mean, the image you're looking for. But today, I'm sorry. That file has been checked out. And," he referred to his screen, "it's an extended loan. Won't be back for four more weeks."

Ruby bit back a groan. Nathan stuffed his hands in his pockets.

The librarian smiled. "You could always try Googling it. The public archives won't have anything on it. They knew we had the extensive file, so would refer people to us. I'm sorry about that. I'm happy to put you down as the next people to check the file out, once it's returned."

Ruby shook her head. "Thanks anyway but we need it now. Wikipedia isn't very complete. And the Tourism P.E.I. website's PDF brochure about the seal isn't too extensive either. We need the file."

The reference librarian swivelled his rolling chair in their direction. "You know." He tapped a pencil against the desktop. "If you're looking for things related to Washington, and Edwina Belliveaux, the public archives *do* have all Edwina's personal diaries. They're just across the way in the Coles building. They have a little less straightforward filing system than we do here. But you said you're a librarian yourself, correct?"

Ruby nodded.

"So I'm sure you'll catch on quick." He smiled and scribbled down the details for her before he handed her the yellow Post-it.

"Thanks." She took the sticky note and glanced at her watch. They'd only been there ten minutes. She and Nathan headed out of the building and crossed the lush green lawn to the Honourable George Coles Building, made of reddish island sandstone. Oaks dotted the expanse of lawn—their notched leaves waved in the light breeze.

"Since you like history," Nathan said, and nodded toward a large Neoclassical stone building on their left, "you should take a look inside Province House. It's where talks were held in the 1860s to create Canada as we know it today. And it's where the Legislative Assembly meets. Kind of like the state capitol buildings in the U.S."

A gaggle of tourists snapped photos on the steps of the building Nathan indicated, its Ionic columns bathed in warm summer sun.

"Archives are up on the third floor, miss," the bald security guard said, after Ruby and Nathan had walked inside the Coles building. "How are ya, Nathan?"

"Good, good. You?"

The guard nodded. "Pretty fair." He waved aside Ruby's attempts to show her photo ID, as the sign requested. "I know you two aren't going to steal anything." He chuckled as he turned back to his computer and his game of solitaire on the screen.

They took the rickety elevator. Its doors slid open with a squeak of protest as it arrived on the third floor. Ruby hurried through the doors as if the elevator might change its mind at any moment.

The door on her right read Public Archives and Records Office of Prince Edward Island.

"I'm just going to run to the washroom," Nathan said, and nodded to a door at the end of the hall.

"Okay," Ruby said, "I'll be in the archives office." She stepped through the door into a small, low-ceilinged room. A wall of windows bathed the room in natural light, and a giant philodendron plant sat on the desk by the door.

"Hi, how are ya?" A late 30-something woman with a round face, blue eyes and short curly brown hair sat behind the desk. Ruby cocked her head. Something about her eyes looked familiar.

"Oh, I'm good. I'm Ruby Zalonski. I'm looking for information about a woman named Edwina Belliveaux."

"Ruby, hi!" The woman smiled. "I'm Evie. It's great to meet you in person."

"Oh, hi, Evie! Nice to meet you too." Ruby smiled back at her.

"So. Edwina Belliveaux." Evie tapped her manicured fingernail against her chin for a second, then turned and dug around in a filing cabinet. "We have all her diaries here." She stepped behind a partition and reappeared a few minutes later with a cardboard banker's box.

"You can take a look at these. It should give you everything you need."

"Thanks, Evie." Nathan said, as he came into the room and stood beside Ruby. "We weren't able to find anything on Google about this. Or at the library." Nathan took the box from his sister and headed across the room to a long, low oak table surrounded by wooden office chairs.

"Nathan?" Evie blinked and looked from Ruby over to Nathan. Ruby just nodded.

"He *never* does this," Evie said to Ruby, as she leaned forward in a conspiratorial whisper. "It's like he's allergic to history. He and our dad didn't see eye to eye on that stuff."

"Really?" Ruby said, and blushed, as she glanced at Nathan over her shoulder. Had he taken the time to do this just for her?

Her heart fluttered. That was sweet of him. But wait. He wasn't doing this for her. He was doing this for his dad. To clear his name.

"So," Evie said, "you're looking for more information about Edwina?"

"Yes, we are. And George Washington. We're trying to find that order."

Evie nodded. "I was there in the lawyer's office too. Dad wouldn't forge anything. But maybe you'll find something about it in Edwina's diaries." She handed Ruby two pairs of white cotton gloves.

"Some sort of connection. Anyway, good luck."

"Thanks," Ruby said, before she joined Nathan at the table and handed him a pair of gloves. He slipped his on and she put on hers.

Then they lifted the lid of the box together. Inside, a series of small, squarish sea-green leather bound books were neatly stacked.

She picked up the first one and eased open the cover. The first page was filled with neat, flowing handwriting, with flourishes and the occasional inkblot.

Charlotte Town 1 May, 1775

Found the most exquisite silk for my new gown. Shall stitch it myself. Perfect for Governor's ball two weeks hence. Shall secure an invitation at once.

Ruby turned the page. More of the same. She flipped to the back of the diary. Again, more entries about ribbon and how many cross-stitch samplers Edwina had embroidered. And how many silver coins she'd given to the poor.

Ruby withheld a sigh. There had to be something in here somewhere...

Nathan picked up the next diary. "More of the same."

Ruby rubbed the back of her neck, and raised her head to ease the tension. She shifted in the hard wooden seat but returned her eyes to the faded writing.

She frowned. Flipped more pages. There was nothing here.

Slowly, they made their way through all the diaries.

She checked the time on her phone. Had they been here nearly three hours? She got up. "Might as well copy some of these entries before we go. If nothing else, they'd be good reference material."

Nathan nodded, and began to put the diaries back neatly into the boxes.

After she'd jotted some notes, Nathan stood. Ruby fought back another surge of disappointment. Had this all been a waste of time?

She clutched her jotted notes on their walk back down Great George Street to Cross Keys Condos.

She looked around. "It's so beautiful here. You know, I heard once that people who are drawn to certain places have lived there in past lives."

Nathan made a noncommittal sound.

"So," Ruby said after a beat of silence,

"what do *you* know about Edwina?"

"Bits and pieces of what Dad would talk about. Edwina was an important citizen. For a woman. Er, at that time, I mean." He raised his hands. "Uh, I'm all for equality."

"I should hope so." Ruby pushed up her glasses.

Nathan cleared his throat. "Well, there's a story that was passed down through the generations—something about how her father or her mother or someone in her family gave away some priceless heirloom to save themselves from being deported." He shook his head. "Only, it didn't work."

"Oh. I thought she'd just said that one famous quote."

"No. She was deported—well, her family was—after the British signed the Treaty of Paris in 1763 and took over P.E.I."

"But she wasn't?"

"That's the thing. There *is* a record of her death at Fort Amherst, in December of 1775." Nathan paused. "But there's a bit of a gap in the history. That was something my father was trying to figure out. In his spare time when he wasn't too busy ignoring his family and his marriage to go off and chase some obscure reference to something that could mean something to someone. Mostly, to him." Nathan's jaw tightened and his gaze shifted to a faraway look.

"But despite all that," Nathan went on, "pretty much everyone on the island tries to claim some relation to Edwina Belliveaux. Kind of like how they do with Lucy Maude Montgomery." He chuckled.

"They do?"

Nathan nodded. A gleam of pride shone in his eyes.

"And speaking of early island history, did you know that Phillips Callbeck, that guy who got kidnapped when the seal was stolen, has descendants that still live on P.E.I.?"

He paused and laughed to himself. "I don't know why I'm telling you this. Or why, really, I remember all of it." He shrugged. "I don't even care about history, really."

"WHY DON'T YOU?" Ruby said, and blinked once. Then again. Nathan felt heat crawl up his torso. He watched Ruby lift her gaze to his. Noticed the tip of her tongue protruded from between her lips. He wet his own.

His mind flicked back to them standing

in the alcove in Dad's study earlier that day. The way she'd felt in his arms.

All at once, he wanted to wrap her up in his embrace, keep her safe and warm and reassure her that nothing, nothing, would ever cause her harm or fear or sadness or pain. That he *would* be there for her.

What the hell?

He stepped backward and banged his heel against the wrought iron bench behind them.

The shock of pain was a welcome relief from the turmoil and tangle of desire and fierce protectiveness that had filled him only moments before.

Was he going crazy?

Nathan swallowed hard and didn't trust himself to speak for a moment.

"But the history gets in your blood, I guess." Nathan shook his head. "This place isn't really like anywhere else." He held up a hand. "I know, I know, that's clichéd to say. And probably doesn't make any sense. But family legacy and history play a big role here. Even though this is the 21st century." His lips pursed.

"When I got off the plane, I had the oddest sense, that I'd been here before. I'd love to live here. Maybe after I complete my Ph.D., I can come back and see the sights." She sighed. "I wish I wasn't adopted," Ruby blurted, her gaze moving back up to his face. He caught his breath at the sight of tears that glimmered in her eyes.

"Why does that bother you?"

She jerked back. "Bother me? It doesn't—" She bit her lip, averted her gaze. "Okay, maybe it does. But I've never felt like I fit in, somehow." She twirled a lock of hair around her finger then pushed her glasses further up her nose.

Nathan held his breath, careful not to stand too close. He didn't want to scare her.

So he simply waited.

She spoke again. "I don't know why that is. I don't know if everyone who's adopted feels this way. And somehow I feel guilty about it. Because my adoptive parents love me. But I always had this...hunger...deep down, to find out more. To know more. To discover, really, who I am. That's why I went into archival studies. So I could, guilt-free, look into other people's pasts and maybe find the answers to my own." She studied her hands. Nathan had to suppress the urge to place his on top of hers.

"I know what you mean," he said.

She cut her gaze to his.

He nodded to her unasked question. "I never belonged." He rubbed a hand across his jaw. "All my life people judged me, just because of my family name. Just because I didn't know what I wanted to do for the rest of my life. Just because I wasn't like every other goddamn O'Neil on this island."

He hadn't realized Ruby had put her hand on his arm until he felt the gentle squeeze. He looked into her hazel eyes and felt the pull of empathy for her situation, mirrored in his own gaze.

He felt a cord of longing inside his heart stretch to nearly the breaking point as he studied the green, gold and caramel-brown flecks of color in her eyes. Suddenly he wanted to unburden himself to her. To tell her all his dark secrets. As if, in simply speaking them, a light would shine so brightly on the darkness that he'd finally be set free. By the mere act of being witnessed by another human being who cared. His lips parted in wonder.

Someone did care. She cared. At least, she would listen to him. Wanted, it seemed, to hear what he had to say. He felt his heart swell.

The silence grew between them.

He rubbed the back of his neck. Started to walk down the sidewalk again.

They'd arrived at the condo. "Anyway, I'm sure you have things to do. Have a good afternoon."

"No, wait." Ruby reached out and put a hand on his arm. "We haven't figured out anything out about the seal...I could use your thoughts, actually." She twirled a strand of hair around her finger.

"Just my thoughts?" Nathan raised a brow as they headed back upstairs.

"You know what I mean," Ruby said, with a laugh.

BUT BACK IN the study, after a few more hours that turned up nothing, Ruby tugged at the end of her ponytail in frustration. "There has to be something here. But there isn't." She dropped her chin into her upturned palm.

Nathan got up. He strode over to his dad's desk, opened the third drawer from the bottom, and reached inside.

Something crinkled as he pulled his hand back out. "I find a candy bar's always a good excuse to take a break. Do you like white chocolate Hershey bars?"

"They're my favorite."

Nathan laughed. "Mine too." He opened one then handed it to her. Took another one for himself. "These Hershey bars were about the only thing Dad and I could agree on."

"That bad, huh?"

Nathan just nodded, and sat on the floor, then leaned back against the mahogany of his dad's desk. He stretched out his legs and crossed one ankle over the other. He broke off a piece of chocolate and chewed.

Ruby got up and joined him. Neither spoke. The only sound was the ticking of the grandfather clock against the opposite wall. Dust motes floated in a sunbeam.

Finally, Nathan broke the silence. "You know..." He mused. "Someone sketched the seal before it was stolen. Remember what the reference librarian said?"

He jumped up and began pacing. "Now I remember Dad mentioned that too. He even had a copy of it, actually. But God knows where it is."

Nathan stopped his pacing and snapped his fingers. "Wait a minute." He picked up a file on his dad's desk and thumbed through it. "I remember Dad saying something about—getting really excited about it—some museum in London had a duplicate of the seal. Well, not a duplicate exactly...I don't remember."

But Ruby was already typing. She turned her laptop to face him. "Do you mean the University of London Library's Fuller Collection? Says on their website that it's not a duplicate. It's a similar one."

She navigated the site. "Look at this!" She pointed. "Someone in that library decided to note that P.E.I. had a similar seal. So then they uploaded a scan of that 1700s diplomat's sketch showing both sides of P.E.I.'s seal."

He pointed to the image. "On the one side there's a large acorn-bearing oak tree beside a smaller oak, with a trunk that divides into three. Says here that it represents P.E.I.'s relationship to England as a colony. England sort of watched over it like an older sibling. And on the other side of the seal was the king's armorial bearings. Basically, his coat of arms. Plus some Latin inscriptions that I won't attempt to pronounce."

Ruby zoomed in to make the sketch as large as possible. She cocked her head. "What are we looking for, here?"

Nathan started to pace again. "I have no

idea. The first clue didn't say much about *what* to look for. Just to look at the seal."

"Hmmm." Ruby scanned the screen, and felt Nathan's breath on her neck as he leaned in to look at the screen too. A shiver slid down her spine.

"Well, logically, it can't be something too complicated. Because the seal isn't very big. The size and shape of a large, heavy coin."

"Right," Ruby said. "And it would have to have been something that could be done quickly. Easily."

"And unobtrusively," Nathan added.

Ruby nodded. "Something that the person leaving the clue and the person picking up on the clue, would both understand."

Nathan didn't respond. He pointed instead to the screen. "What are those marks?" He tilted his head.

"Let's see if I can zoom in a bit more... Oh, around the edge of the seal?" She tapped a finger against her chin. "They just look like strike marks. When they made it."

"No," Nathan said, "they're too regular for that... Too uniform." He leaned even nearer to Ruby. Her heart sped up.

She jumped to her feet. "Here. It seems like you need to sit down. Have my seat."

He glanced at her, held her gaze for a moment longer than necessary, then sat. "You don't need to be afraid of me, you know." He paused. "I don't bite."

Ruby gave a shaky laugh. "Of course not." She tightened her ponytail. "I was just giving you more room."

He caught Ruby's eye and winked. "You know," he said, "the last time I had to sort through documents and do some research was at UPEI. After hours. In the library stacks. Somehow I ended up making out with my research partner. Got an F on the assignment. But I did enjoy myself." His eyes twinkled.

Ruby gave him a playful shove on the shoulder. "Well, that's not the kind of research we're doing here."

He held her gaze. "You sure about that?" His tone turned serious.

Ruby shifted her weight and crossed her arms. The ticking of the grandfather clock sounded loud to her ears.

She cleared her throat. The man was too perceptive for his own good. How did he *do* that? Interpret her in ways she could barely begin to admit to herself?

She turned back to the screen and ignored the way her heart pounded. She was leaving. In three days. Couldn't get involved. And she wasn't going to just have a fling—she wasn't the type. She cleared her throat. "So what do you think it is?"

"Numbers," he said, and traced a finger along the edge. "But not Arabic numbers. See the repetition of marks? The vertical lines. These are—"

"Roman numerals." Ruby grinned. "Nice job!"

Nathan leaned back in the computer chair and looked up at her over his shoulder. "We make a pretty good team."

Ruby smiled back. Held his gaze as she held her breath. Somehow, she found herself move forward ever so slightly. What would it be like to lean in, reach up, run her fingers along his jawline, press her lips against his—

The ding of an incoming message on Ruby's phone made her jump. She glanced at it.

Maggie wanted to know how the hunt was going. And wondered just where things were at with a certain Nathan O'Neil. Ruby tapped back a 'talk soon' reply, then turned to Nathan. "But what do the Roman numerals mean?"

"Well, assuming we're looking for another riddle, the numbers are obviously some sort of clue. So..." Nathan trailed off.

"Let's think about what we already know," Ruby said. "That first clue referred to the compass. And then General Washington. And lastly to the seal. But I don't get how the Roman numerals fit in."

Nathan pushed away from the desk suddenly and stood. "Why didn't I see it before? It's a cipher. The numbers are a cipher. But which one?" He ran a hand through his hair.

"There are so many codes and ciphers..." Ruby rubbed her temples. Then stifled a yawn and checked her watch. "I can't believe we've been up here for this long. It's practically 10 p.m." She sighed. "You'd have to memorize whole books to know stuff like that."

"I got a book like that for Christmas once," Nathan said, and glanced at the screen again. "But this points to a specific cipher because the numerals are in sets of three. It's a book cipher. Technically," Nathan tilted his head. "...it's called an Ottendorf cipher."

Ruby laughed softly. "How do you *know* this?"

"I spent time reading that code book—plus a few more—back when I'd been unemployed for months. Dad knew I loved logic and rational thinking. Math. That sort of thing. I think he gave me that code book because he might've been getting a little desperate in hoping I'd get a good job. He joked I should join CSIS." Nathan chuckled. "It's the Canadian version of the FBI," he said, in response to the questioning look in Ruby's gaze.

"Wow, you know something I don't," Ruby couldn't help teasing.

A sparkle gleamed in Nathan's eye. "Maybe more than one thing." He leveled his gaze on her.

She blushed and changed the subject. "Right. So what's an Ottendorf cipher?"

"It's a series of three numbers used to reference a document that contains a code. That's the beauty of it. You can use any written document—even the dictionary— as a way to convey a secret message. So the way the numbers work—the first one refers to a page. The second number refers to a line. And the third number refers to a word on that line in the document."

"Okay. That sounds simple enough. But which document?"

"Hmm, good question." Nathan began pacing. "Well, it needs to be old. In the same era as the seal."

Ruby nodded. "And it needs to be...official, probably. Historically significant."

"Wait. In the first clue... It talked about *Goodhearted General's Orders did put forth—*" Nathan met her gaze.

"You're right," Ruby said. "That means we need to use this Ottendorf cipher on Washington's orders."

Ruby stifled another yawn and glanced at her watch again.

"We can call it a night for now, though. But can we meet back here tomorrow after I'm done with some things at the office, and keep going?"

Ruby nodded. "Sounds good."

After Nathan left, inside the condo bedroom, Ruby changed into her oversized sleeping shirt. She belted a light robe around her waist and glanced out the door leading to the small balcony overlooking the back of St. Dunstan's cathedral and Gahan House restaurant.

Her hand was on the doorknob before she realized it.

She stepped out onto the small balcony. The amber glow of fairy lights strung across the outdoor patio of the restaurant combined with the scent of bright red potted geraniums and the murmur of the diners. She exhaled softly and closed her eyes. So peaceful. She found herself leaning against the wrought iron railing.

Warm summer air blew across her face and she breathed a sigh of contentment. What was it about this place that had her feeling so at home?

She pursed her lips.

She headed back to the bedroom and fell asleep as soon as her head hit the pillow.

He ran to her down the forest trail. Her heart lifted, the sting of sea salt on her cheeks, the scent of wild roses in her hair.

He neared her. She could see the shine of the brass buckles on the strap of the leather artist's bag slung across his chest, over the forest green wool of his great coat. The coat that her fingers had brushed over many a time in these late summer evenings with the tang of salt in the air and the taste of his skin on her lips.

Oh, how she longed to stroke her fingers along the length of that strong, sturdy leather. To feel the broad width of his shoulders under her palms, the scratchy wool of his jacket, the rough scrape of his stubble against her. Everywhere.

She whispered his name, those well-loved

syllables—

"Alexander," the name jerked Ruby awake. Even as she spoke the word, half-awake, half-asleep, she felt as if rust and saltwater coated her throat.

Ruby swallowed, then startled fully awake. Because in the strange manner of dreams, he had had Nathan's face.

Chapter Five

SATURDAY MORNING LIGHT slanted through the large plate-glass windows at Island Design & Tech. Nathan sat at a glass and chrome desk in the southeast corner. A few of his colleagues sat at their desks, too.

He executed the last few keystrokes on his Mac and then sat back in the white office chair, his fingers steepled as he studied the rendering on the screen. Pretty good.

He cocked his head. There was something missing from the design. He narrowed his eyes at the image on the screen.

Hmmm. He tapped his fingers on the chair arm. What was it? No. The lines were fine. And the perspective was good... He tilted his head to the other side.

Of course. He sat forward. The shading. He made a few adjustments with the keyboard. A surge of satisfaction pulsed through him. There. That was exactly right.

Just then, his phone rang. He picked it up. "Nathan," his boss said, "since you're working today, just wanted to check in and ask how the new logo's coming?"

Nathan grinned. "Just finished it." Without thinking, he picked up one of the freshly sharpened No. 2 pencils he kept in one of his mother's glass jam jars at the top right-hand corner of his desk and, out of long habit, began to sketch absently as he talked. "I'll send you a proof in a minute."

"Good." His boss continued. "See you Monday."

"Sure," Nathan said then hung up the phone. He glanced down at the page in front of him. His hand froze as he stared at the sketch.

Ringlets of perfectly curled hair fell to the woman's shoulders, and the square neckline of the pale pink silk dress she wore revealed her to be from the 1700s.

And behind her, drawn in hurried strokes, was a waning moon with a wind-blown chestnut tree and the hasty outline of a man astride a horse.

But it was the slight smile that touched the woman's half-formed lips, as she looked up at the man that held Nathan's gaze. Because it was the same woman he'd painted...which meant it was Edwina Belliveaux. Again.

Nathan stared at the pencil in his hand and willed it to stop trembling. But he couldn't make his fingers stop shaking. Or his heart stop pounding.

Because her large green eyes—they seemed...familiar somehow. His mind flitted back to the way Ruby had looked at him yesterday at the archives.

At the eager, excited expression on her face when she'd found that letter fragment. He grinned, but it quickly faded. There was such a sadness and frustration in her gaze when they hadn't found out anything more about Edwina. He sighed. What could he do to help her? He had to do something. Ease her burden.

People who are drawn to places have lived there before. Ruby's words flashed through his mind. Was that true for events, too?

No. These drawings were just some ramblings of his subconscious mind, what with all the talk they'd been doing about Edwina.

That was all. Just doodlings, transferred onto paper.

Besides, Ruby was an academic. He would have thought she'd be more grounded than to believe in those sorts of New Age things.

Looked like she was just as much a romantic as his father had been. He had to keep his distance. Good thing she was leaving soon. His attraction to her would fade when she was gone.

All the more reason to stay away from her. At least as much as he could, what with them still working together to find that damn order. He couldn't afford to be disappointed in love again. So why was he more interested in her than he had been in any other woman he'd met?

He shook his head and glanced down at the sketch again. No. Her eyes weren't green. He hadn't colored them in. And her dress wasn't pink. He hadn't shaded that in, either. He crumpled up the sketch. What the hell was going on?

He'd always loved drawing. But in university, when deciding his degree path, he chose a double degree: business and graphic design. For the simple fact that his parents had agreed to pay for his education if he stayed on P.E.I. But if he'd followed his passion and gone to art school off island, he would've had to pay for it himself.

So he'd done the practical thing. Even if it had broken his heart in the process.

He shook his head at himself. He was perfectly happy in his job. Wasn't he? He wasn't miserable or broke.

He couldn't keep doing this. Keep thinking he'd made some mistake over and over when he had a good job with good pay in a place he loved.

He studied the pencil lines, the shading, the use of light. He frowned. Maybe he should've gone to art school after all. He carefully folded the paper and tucked it into his pants pocket.

Nathan shook off his thoughts and turned his attention back to the logo design in front of him.

RUBY HAD MADE quite a bit of progress on the cataloging that morning, so she decided to head over to the boardwalk along Victoria Park.

She watched the mid-morning sun sparkle off of the bay. The occasional caw of a crow intermingled with the cry of a seagull as they fought over some French fries and half-open wild mussel shells scattered on the rocky shoreline along the winding boardwalk of Charlottetown's waterfront.

She didn't want to leave now. Ruby chewed on a corner of her thumbnail. But who knew when she'd get another interview for a job as perfect as that?

Sailboats bobbed on the calm waters, and the occasional jet-ski buzzed by. But mostly, she had the place to herself. Only a few dog walkers and joggers were out this time of day.

She'd found the other half of the love letter fragment. And that was great. She grinned. She'd already started adding it into her research.

But she still had so many questions. For instance, what had happened to Edwina? What had she been up to? And what else had happened between her and Alexander?

Maybe there weren't any more love letters at all...

Ruby inhaled the scents of sea salt and pine trees as she walked past the long-needle pines whose limbs grew at fantastical angles that reminded her of something out of Dr. Seuss.

She grinned. Those had been some of her favorite books as a child. And she thought she could recite pretty much every sentence from every one of his books.

Her eyes darted to a long outdoor line-up as she passed a small wooden building painted yellow with blue shutters. The words dairy bar were done in block letters above the gingerbread scrollwork of the front porch. She'd have to stop for ice cream another time. She chewed on her other thumbnail.

Was Edwina a spy? And who was this Alexander person? The 'young man whose name has been lost to history' that Dr. O'Neil had mentioned in his emails to her? Not only that, what about that dream she'd had? Did it have anything to do with all of this? Have any basis in reality? Not that she could exactly use it as a primary source...

Ruby kept walking along the wooden boardwalk. She spotted a lighthouse at the far end and couldn't help smiling.

It was painted a bright white with a red stripe near the top. It seemed to watch over the quiet scene, perched there on a pile of red sandstone outcropped against the blue waters of the harbor.

Despite everything, she felt a thrill run through her. She was really here. On Prince Edward Island. She'd make it. She'd prevail, no matter what it took.

Her thoughts flicked to Nathan for a moment. He'd been very helpful. Was Evie right? She'd definitely implied Nathan wanted to spend time with her. Ruby's heart pounded.

But was he just being nice? Just serving his own ends, wanting to find the order so that his dad's name could be cleared? Did he *really* want to spend time with her? Someone that attractive... With that kind of past...

But then she remembered the look in his eyes as he'd given the money to the homeless man. The way her heart had melted, just a little, when he'd asked her if he could come by again. Or that feeling of...what? ...when they'd been together in the alcove. And then again on the street. How she'd opened up to him. The way she'd just wanted to melt into his arms when he'd read that fragment.

She frowned. If she didn't find out exactly what was going on with Edwina, and with the love letter, not to mention finish sorting through the rest of Dr. O'Neil's papers, then not only would her dissertation have to be significantly rewritten, but she'd lose the edge she needed for the job application.

Just then, Ruby's phone rang. She glanced at it. Dr. Burton.

"Listen, Ruby. Are you back in town yet?"

"No, why? I just booked my flight—I get in Sunday."

A pause. "Listen, Ruby. I'm really not supposed to be telling you this." Dr. Burton lowered her voice. "But these are special circumstances, what with the investigation into Dr. O'Neil's research. Someone on the committee who's reviewing your dissertation defense says that your research is suspect. That means you'll need to have rock-solid primary sources prepped for it."

"What? How? But everyone approved it initially."

"I know." Dr. Burton sighed. "Seems one of them read something online about this whole inquest into Dr. O'Neil's research. And since you were corresponding with him, well, it's reflecting badly on you and your research."

Ruby chewed her lip. "But—" If only Dr. O'Neil hadn't left things in such a mess. They hadn't even been able to find that psalm book he'd mentioned in his email to her. Of course, even if they had, he had obviously already taken the order out of it.

"I know, Ruby. I don't like it either. Please, just get back here as soon as you can."

"Okay," Ruby said. "Thanks for telling me." She ended the call.

She reached the lighthouse at the end of the boardwalk. She paused to watch puffy clouds sail across a blue sky. Then she turned around and headed back to the condo and let herself in.

She sank down onto a stool by the door to take off her tennis shoes and then headed to the bathroom and splashed cold water on her face.

After she towelled off, she raised her head. She wouldn't stop until she had the answers she was seeking. There was always an answer. Always a solution.

Even though she had no clue what that was right now.

"HI NATHAN," RUBY said, as he walked into his dad's study Saturday afternoon.

She'd just logged onto her Simmons College email provider and printed out the first order. Her laptop screen flickered. "Okay, so I'll print out the whole thing. Just to be safe. Because even though Washington only refers to Canada in the very last paragraph of this order, who knows? Maybe the rest of the message is in the other part."

"Good thinking."

Ruby waited for the printer to spit out the page. She frowned as the computer's screen flickered again, and the laptop made a choked whirring noise. "So," Ruby said, "this is what we have." She took the page and turned to Nathan.

"Okay," he said. "Let's apply these Roman numerals."

"But how do we know if we're starting in the right place?" Ruby asked.

She set the still-warm sheet down on Dr. O'Neil's desk and she and Nathan looked at it. "Well," he said, "actually, that's simple. There is only one page to this order, so we know that first number would be a one. These other numbers that come after are too high."

"That makes sense."

"The second number is the line..." Nathan counted down the number of lines on the order. "Okay," he tapped a finger. "Here."

"And what's the third number again? Oh right, the word in the line." Ruby counted over. "'Hearts'" is the first word."

She grabbed a yellow legal pad and wrote that in neat block letters.

"Looks like 'of' is the next one." Nathan picked up the pen and wrote that down beside Ruby's word.

"And..." Ruby's eyes scanned the page, "'ink' comes after that."

Nathan picked up the pen again after Ruby had written down *ink* and wrote down three more words.

Ruby glanced at the pad. "You're good at that."

Nathan shrugged. "Practice, I guess. All those months of unemployment I had to do something." He grinned. "So it looks like we have our first sentence."

Ruby read it aloud. *"Hearts of ink/Sealed in highest wooden frame, where—*' That's not the whole thing, though."

"But that's all the numbers for this page. There are other numbers but it must refer to a different page."

"No, not just a different page. A different order. The rest of the message is in the other order. And I bet it's the one that Washington sent about Edwina. That makes the most sense." Ruby grinned. "I have the second order right—"

But when she turned back to her screen, it was completely black. No amount of rebooting would revive it.

"Your computer's dead," Nathan said.

"But you're the computer expert. Can't you just fix it?"

"It's too far gone for that."

Ruby chewed a cuticle. "Now what? We need to look at that second order." She slumped back in her seat. "And my email software client was the only way to get a look at that. That is, unless we somehow stumble upon the original your dad had around here somewhere." She glanced around. Sighed. "This feels impossible all of a sudden."

"Hey," Nathan said softly. Put a hand on her shoulder. "Something's bound to work out. But in the meantime, have you walked along the quay yet?"

Ruby shook her head.

"Come on," Nathan said, "getting some fresh air will maybe give us a new perspective."

A few minutes later, they were walking along the quay. The gray boards creaked and heaved ever so slightly under Ruby's footsteps.

Sailboats bobbed in their moorings, and the blue water sparkled in the afternoon sun. The sounds of an acoustic guitar mixed with the slap of the waves against the pier as a guitarist picked out a melody on the small stage by Peake's Quay.

"Ruby," Nathan said, "don't give up." She looked at him, her eyes wide. Nathan's gaze became serious. "You can't. You've come too far. Literally."

A little girl with blonde braids zipped past their slow amble. A group of tourists, all eating ice cream cones, sat on one of the old-fashioned wooden benches that faced the water.

Ruby gave a shaky laugh. "Well, thanks."

"No," Nathan said, "I mean it. You're determined. Smart. You don't back down. People like that, well, I really..." He cleared his throat. "Admire. Because," he ran a hand through his hair, "I haven't done that. Sure, I'm in graphic design, something I enjoy. But... well, I felt so restricted. By Dad. By expectations." He sighed. Then spotted a bench tucked into a quiet corner and sat.

Ruby sat too and waited for him to continue.

He looked out over the harbor. "Truth is, I feel like I've settled, with my job. And maybe even with my life." He raised his eyes to her.

She found herself leaning forward, wanting to reassure him. Somehow. "Well, what would you like to do? If you could?"

Nathan reached into his jeans pocket and pulled out a neatly folded piece of lined paper and handed it to Ruby. Its edges fluttered in the soft breeze as she unfolded it.

Ruby traced a finger along the pencil lines. "She's so lifelike. The way you've captured her eyes..." Ruby's own eyes widened. "That's the same woman in my locket picture. She looks...wow. For what it's worth, Nathan, you have got talent."

Nathan blinked rapidly a couple of times. "Thank you." He took a breath. "No one's ever said that to me before." He put a hand over Ruby's and squeezed.

"My family situation, well...Dad and I had a huge fight," Nathan continued. His blue eyes were fringed with dark lashes. But as he blinked, Ruby thought for a second that she saw his eyes change color to a caramel brown. And in that instant, she felt a pull of recognition, familiarity. But in the next moment, as he blinked again, his eyes were blue.

She took in a breath. Probably just a trick of the light.

Ruby tried to pay attention to what he was saying. But all she could do was revel in the feelings of desire and open heartedness that welled up in her as he continued to talk. Continued to open up his soul for her. To her.

"I felt terrible about it. And now," he

paused, "there's nothing I can do about it. We were never that close. In fact," he laughed, though there wasn't anything funny, "Mom used to say that we were too much alike. She said that was what our problem was. If you can call it a problem. Maybe it wasn't a problem. Maybe it was simply who we were. Who we are...And now who he'll never be." Nathan studied his hands. Then looked back up at Ruby.

"You know, I've always been like this. Ever since I was little." He rubbed the back of his neck. "I think he thought that I had some sort of predilection for not following the rules. Taking risks and loving it." He gave a quiet laugh. "And if Mom could see me now." He moved his eyes back up to Ruby's. "I don't think she'd be proud of me at all." He swallowed. "Because what am I doing?" His lips twisted. "What am I doing here? I'm 33 and I thought I would've figured that out by now."

He tugged at his earlobe and blinked rapidly a few times.

Ruby held her breath. Let it out slowly. "What is bad, anyway? There are so many shades of gray." And maybe, just maybe, things weren't quite so black and white as she would've liked, about Nathan. "Maybe," she added, "there isn't really bad and good. Maybe everyone has parts of each."

Ruby felt his fingers intertwine with hers.

But the bark of a Scotty dog that trotted by, made Ruby startle and remove her hand. She glanced at her watch, straightened then got up. "Well, I should probably get back. Thanks, though, for...this."

Nathan nodded and stood too. Shoved his hands in his pockets. "Yeah. You're welcome." He sighed. "I guess we have to think of something else, with that order. I need to get home now, but I'll think on it, ok?"

AT HOME THAT night, Nathan flipped through the channels on TV, his mind elsewhere. Ruby was leaving soon. They hadn't found much of anything to do with the order at all. What was he going to do about Dad, then?

His fingers clenched.

He wouldn't give up. Not yet. Not now. He got up and began pacing. His steps led him somehow downstairs to the studio in his basement.

He needed to straighten things up a bit.

He lined up the containers filled with

paints and brushes. Then bent down and picked up a drop-sheet he'd haphazardly placed on top of a coffee table nearby.

Underneath, still bundled in its linen wrappings, was that small leather book. How had it gotten here? Oh, right. He must've brought it down here after he'd had it in the lawyer's office.

Nathan picked it up and drew a thumb across the cracked leather-bound surface. How many years had it lain in the wall? Would this, maybe, be some way to help Ruby out? Even if she was leaving, he did want to help her. It was the decent thing to do.

Had someone stolen it from whoever this person was, and hidden it behind the brick?

Nathan watched the overhead light glint against the faintest gold-leaf remnants that still clung to the front cover.

Why was it blank? A crease appeared between his brows as he flipped pages. The faint scent of citrus wafted to him.

Nathan's pulse sped up. Why go to the trouble of hiding something like this if all the pages were blank? There had to be a reason.

He set the journal back down on the coffee table near his battered old couch and reached for his laptop. Typed 'old journals and citrus' into the search box. It seemed, as he scanned the hits, that citrus was used in the old days to make invisible ink. Hmmm.

Which meant that the pages weren't blank after all, but simply disguised...

After a few minutes of research, he came across a website detailing how to make invisible ink visible.

He went upstairs into his ensuite bathroom and rummaged around in the drawer below the sink. Hmmm. He usually just towel-dried his hair but—Yes. Here it was. He pulled out a hairdryer.

He went to the kitchen, hairdryer in hand and set it on the table. Then he went to the kitchen sink and grabbed a couple of kitchen trash bags from the Glad dispenser below the sink, along with the rubber gloves he used to wash dishes with.

He came back to the kitchen table, spread the new plastic garbage bag out, placed the hairdryer on top, and then pulled on his rubber gloves.

Then he went back down into the basement for the book and went back upstairs into the kitchen. He set it down on the plastic, and opened it to the very first blank page.

He picked up the hairdryer and flicked it onto the lowest setting then held it aloft. Paused. Looked down at the page. Swallowed. Slowly aimed the hairdryer at the surface.

He moved the hair dryer along the antiquated page, in long slow passes. Would this even work? Nothing seemed to be happening.

But he worked his way along the page until the entire surface was heated.

He hoped he wouldn't somehow set it on fire.

He shook his head. What would his father think of him doing this? He chuckled to himself.

He'd probably have a fit. And Ruby? What would she do? She'd thank him, probably. Maybe. If, that is, he found anything in here worthwhile.

He glanced down at the antiquated surface. But the page remained blank.

He frowned. Had he read the instructions wrong? It said to wait for a little while. He pursed his lips and cocked his head. Then again, it was the internet. Maybe the instructions were completely wrong.

He looked up at the clock on the wall. One minute had passed. He looked back down at the page.

Something *was* there.

Nathan's heart pounded. Was this how Ruby and Dad felt every time they discovered something? Nathan grinned. He could see why they kept chasing. Because one thing just might lead to another and if enough time and energy were put in, who knew what might be uncovered.

Nathan studied the page. It looked like... He cocked his head. A date. And two entries. He read the first.

Charlotte Town   3 June 1775

I shall not fail in my second attempt to regain my family's heirloom, as I did when attending Governor Patterson's Ball. He, who bought the compass from Lord Amherst. Oh, how my heart beat when I nearly held its engraved golden surface in my hands in the dark and stillness of Patterson's private offices. I did not count on his fondness for puzzle boxes, else I would have my heirloom even now.

Nor did I believe I would have to explain my uninvited presence to Himself, so I could not gain time to procure my prize. Given I was in the

Governor's private offices, it does stand to reason his demanding an explanation. I could not risk the Governor's suspicions, so while I answered him, I took heart in having hidden my precious heirloom in plainest sight.

I fear to say quite where, even betwixt these pages, for this Book may fall into the Wrong hands. I can only pray that hiding my heirloom in plainest sight, alongside the Seal, will keep it safe until Providence affords me the good fortune of retrieving it.

Nathan then turned to the second entry:

Boston 22 Sept. 1775

Though the commissioners from the Continental Congress in the 13 Colonies have failed to win the French-Canadians to the Cause, W. still has hope, as he told me, that some French-Canadians may be sympathetic to the Patriots and provide Aide to the Rebellion. That is why he is allowing me to join Captains Broughton and Selman on their mission to intercept British ships bound for Quebec along the St. Lawrence River, six weeks hence.

Though 'tis not for W. nor any of the Patriot Cause that I take upon myself this sworn duty, but for myself. And most of All, for my Family. The compass shall be restored to our family. 'Tis, after all, my rightful heirloom.

I shall see to its safe return, no matter what shall befall me. The British did not honor their Word when they deported my family instead of allowing us to stay. But the British will pay. And the compass shall be mine again.

W. has entreated I come aboard ship as Cook. IIe assured me of my safety and that none would be the wiser as to the true emissary nature of my mission with the French-Canadians. So he thinks. I pray it be so...

Before we sail, I shall make my way to Mr. Revere the Silversmith at his shop on Clark's Wharf to fetch the locket he has crafted specially.

Nathan pulled out a chair. Was there more? Only one way to find out. He flicked on the hairdryer again and set to work.

He grinned. Ruby would love this. He had to show it to her. He could give it to her. This would definitely help her research about the love letters, which was, apparently, connected to Washington and the order. And to the seal.

Maybe he could trust Ruby not to put her career before...whatever this blossoming connection was between them. And maybe Dad hadn't been so crazy, after all. Which meant Ruby had never been, either...

THAT EVENING, RUBY stepped out of the shower and wrapped herself in her robe. Glasses in hand, she started to thread her way through the chaos of the partially renovated living room, on her way back to the bedroom.

Her heart felt like a helium balloon. As if it would just lift off and float up into the sky. Into the blue, blue sky. The same blue as Nathan's eyes.

She grinned. Nathan.

She hummed as she wove around the haphazard stacks of drywall, buckets of mudding mix, and ladders. She coughed as her footsteps stirred up dust.

As she wiped her eyes after she finished coughing, she tripped over the bucket of drywall mud. She caught her balance, but the glasses she carried went flying.

They landed in a large hole the contractors had made when they'd ripped away the old plaster. She crouched down near the large bucket and studied the hole in the plaster.

She took a deep breath and shoved aside the heavy bucket. Slowly, Ruby put her hand inside the hole to retrieve her glasses. She hoped there weren't any spiders.

Mildew, dust and the faintest hint of wild roses greeted her as she leaned in close to the hole. She sneezed.

Her heart pounded.

But instead of a smooth plastic glasses frame, her fingers encountered something scratchy and warm. It felt like...a wool blanket?

She moved her fingers forward. There were her glasses.

Curious, she drew out a moth-eaten green wool saddle blanket, along with the glasses. She unfolded the blanket. Inside, bound with a frayed pink ribbon, was a single tattered letter. Her heart sped up. Had that Molly person stashed it here?

She flipped over the thick paper. The wax seal was still intact.

She hesitated only a moment before she slid her finger under the wax and lifted.

St. John's Island   14 Dec. 1775

Edwina, my love,

I have received your latest missive and do not know where to begin, so I shall at the heart of the matter.

You voiced your concern over the actions you took on Nov. 17 in Charlotte Town when you absconded with not only the Seal, but also with me.

Yet what other way was there for you to fight back against those who stole your Property than in the manner of your upbringing?

The British, and these so-called Colonists, forced your People out. It was only natural, your desire to stay on that island's shores. After all, 'twas your homeland before the British claimed it.

Do not fret, my darling. We need to trust that the Compass shall reu-

*nite us. You have told me of its pow-
ers to do just that. Have you not
regaled me with tales of its powers
working throughout the generations
of your family? And that was why it
was such a precious Heirloom?*

*The British knew not what they
took from you. But your father, in
attempting and failing to barter your
family's Freedom, with the sale of the
compass to Lord Amherst, did. Yet he
only thought he was doing what was
Right.*

*Do not lose hope, beloved. All at
last shall be set to rights.*

*Your Faithful Servant
Alexander*

Ruby's eyes widened. The *sale* of the
compass? She tapped a finger against her
chin. That family heirloom tale Nathan
mentioned... So there was truth behind
that legend, too. A smile curved Ruby's
lips.

She cocked her head.

All those receipts she'd gone
through...Wait a second. There'd been a
crumbling old bill of exchange for a
compass. Hadn't there?

She scrambled to her feet. She headed into Dr. O'Neil's study and plucked up the pile of receipts she'd sorted. Here it was.

Her heart pounded. Nathan could use this to help clear Dr. O'Neil's name. It wasn't the second order, but at least it would help people believe the late professor wasn't a crackpot.

She straightened up and looked back at the letter. She turned it over. Held it up. But as she did, she paused.

It looked as if—she cocked her head and peered more closely.

Underneath the flourishes and ink splatters of the original words, various letters had tiny dots under them. In a random order. No. Not random at all. It was a coded message:

Compass rose sheds its light in the rose-red moonlight —A

OUT OF THE corner of her eye, Ruby saw Nathan walk through the study doorway on Sunday morning. He dusted off his jeans and approached her. Ruby smoothed a stray curl behind her ear. She was leaving tonight. She swallowed down a lump in her throat.

Where had he been? She darted a glance at her watch. He was supposed to have been here more than 30 minutes ago. She tamped down a flicker of irritation.

"Sorry I'm late," he said. "Had to go pay a speeding ticket."

"Oh." She couldn't pretend she wasn't disappointed. The flicker of annoyance grew. She forced it back.

Nathan extended a handful of documents to her. "I'm not quite sure what they all are. But I hope it might give us some hints about where the order might be."

He yawned but tried to hide it behind the fistful of papers. "I found them in Dad's car." He shook his head. "He liked to file things *everywhere*. Kept his mind sharp, so he said."

"Thanks." Ruby took the documents from him. Her stomach dipped. She wouldn't get to see him again, if she went back to Boston and took that job. If the interview went well and they offered it to her, anyway. Her heart hammered. Her palms felt clammy. She couldn't lose him. What? She shook her head and forced herself to take a breath. She wasn't losing him. She was leaving. This was her choice. Her life. Her career.

Just then she noticed his bloodshot eyes. "Are you hung over?" She bit her lip. *Still acting like a teenager*—the women's words echoed in her ears. Maybe it was a good thing she was going.

But Nathan just chuckled. "Yeah. Friend's bachelor party last night." He yawned again. Shook his head. "Been having strange dreams for about two weeks solid, which hasn't helped either."

He rubbed his chest. "I'm getting too old for that kind of late night. But at least I have my jalepeño cream cheese bagel to tide me over." He held up a paper bag with the Great Canadian Bagel logo emblazoned across it. "Want one?"

She winced. That bag might've been near some irreplaceable documents. The flicker of annoyance surged again.

"Oh, um, no thank you. I don't do spicy things."

"No?" Nathan glanced at her, eyebrows raised. He reached into the bag, pulled out a bagel half and took a bite.

"I, uh," She reached for the container of paperclips but knocked it over. She cleared her throat. "I found a love letter yesterday." She let out a huff of irritation. "But it just leads to more questions. Not answers." She crossed her arms.

"Well, that should be exactly what you want, right?"

She dropped her chin into her hand and looked around. The piles of junk she'd organized. And the random things she'd arranged. They were no longer scattered across the desk surface, the floor, the windows or the built-in bookcase.

Nathan pulled out a small leather-bound book. "I found something interesting." He switched on the lamp on the mahogany desk.

She caught sight of his eager, hopeful expression as she watched him look at her out of the corner of her eye.

She felt a stab of guilt. How could she be judging him like that? He was only trying to help. It was kind of sweet.

"I think it's Edwina's diary, Ruby," he whispered. His breath stirred her hair and sent a shiver down her spine.

"But we just looked at her diaries a few days ago."

"No, I think this is another one. I found it at Fort Amherst. I know how important these documents are to you, and so..." He met her gaze.

She swallowed. Then reached up and put a hand on his arm. "Thank you. You said Fort Amherst?"

Nathan nodded. "Across the harbor. It's a national historic site. Used to be French. And a jail. Anyway," he grinned. "There's a bunch of entries. But I didn't have time last night to read the whole thing. Used a hair dryer to reveal the invisible ink." He flipped the book open. Leaned forward. "See?"

But Ruby leaned back in the cracked leather wingback and chewed on her bottom lip. She avoided Nathan's gaze. "I have a job interview to go to tomorrow," she blurted.

Nathan frowned.

But she hurried on. "And because my research is connected to your dad's, it's being called into question too." She blinked back tears. Took a breath. She *should* be happy he'd found another journal of Edwina's. But somehow, she just felt...afraid, she realized. Afraid that by looking in the journal, she'd find out— what? That things with Nathan would end? But that didn't make any sense. Yet the feeling persisted.

Why was she feeling so overwhelmed all of a sudden? She clutched the locket. No. She wasn't abandoning Nathan. Wasn't leaving him. She took a deep breath. She'd done what she could, here. That was all.

Beside her, Nathan stiffened. Pushed away from the edge of the desk he had leaned against.

Ruby's heart sank to her toes. "I need to go back to Boston. I...I...don't want more clues, more questions. I have to finish things, not start more." She slid the locket chain through her fingers and watched him turn away. A spasm of panic clutched her chest. No. He couldn't just walk away from her. Not after all they'd shared. What? They hadn't shared that much...

Nathan's shoulders tensed. He clenched his jaw and moved into the center of the room.

"I—I need to substantiate what I've found," she continued. "Not hunt down what could be more dead ends."

Nathan's gaze bored into hers.

"So," he said slowly. "You only want that position. Want to further your career." Nathan crossed his arms. "You're leaving me here to fend for myself."

Ruby pushed back from the desk. Looked up at him. "That's not true."

"No?" He raised his eyebrows. "I should have seen it coming. I thought you were...different. But no. You're just like my dad." Nathan shook his head. "That's all you really care about, isn't it—your career."

"No, Nathan," she said. "It's not. I just—"

Nathan started pacing. "We haven't found the order." He shoved a hand through his hair. "My dad's name is about to be mud if we don't, and you're... You're..." He clenched his jaw and his voice rose "—leaving for some damn interview."

"I need to prep for it. Go back to Boston." Ruby fought to keep her voice steady even as the flicker of annoyance came back, hovered just above a sense of panic. Grew.

"Well, maybe you should."

Ruby lifted her chin. "I need to figure out what I'm going to do about my research." She narrowed her eyes. Fought down the panic. "Finish my dissertation. Prep for my defence." She knew she was repeating herself but she couldn't help it.

"No," Nathan said. He paced faster. "You're giving up. Selling out. When all I tried to do was help you. When all I wanted to do was the right thing."

Ruby jumped up. "And you're being completely irrational. You knew I'd be leaving. I knew I'd be leaving. The cataloging is basically done." She tore her gaze away from his icy stare.

"Well, where I come from," he said, voice tight, "a promise to help is a promise. Loyalty means something."

"Oh, don't go pulling that Island heritage crap on me. You're blowing this all out of proportion."

Nathan merely raised his chin.

Ruby gave a huff of irritation. "Fine, Nathan. You want the truth? Here it is. I've come across more than I'd dreamed. Not only that, I've gone through these things. Done my job here. After all, that's what I came here to do." And yet...Her eyes flicked to Nathan. Then back to the last pile of papers. Guilt tore at her. She was leaving him...

"And yet you're still leaving." Nathan ground his teeth. "You know what?" He shoved the diary at Ruby. "Take the journal. Maybe it'll remind you of what you should've done."

Then he turned and left the room. The door rattled as he slammed it.

Chapter Six

OUTSIDE THE CONDO early that evening, Ruby tugged her battered purple suitcase behind her on the sidewalk.

She turned the corner, where the cab was supposed to pick her up, and caught her breath. Golds and pinks of sunset shimmered along the harbor, just visible from her vantage point at the intersection of Queen and Dorchester streets. The evening light touched the red brick facades. Seagulls soared overhead against the background of a few wispy clouds in an otherwise blue sky.

And then she saw Nathan. He leaned against the rough brick wall of the building, his expression impossible to read. Her heart plummeted.

He pushed away from the wall, his jaw clenched. "Thank you for organizing the papers."

"You're welcome," she said in a tight voice. She sought his gaze, as if it might tell her something. But it was unreadable. Yet a ripple of déja vù passed through her and she gripped the handle of her suitcase as sudden images flashed through her mind.

It couldn't be much longer now. She paced back and forth in the tiny cell, the hem of her skirts heavy with rainwater and the tears that seemed endless. She clutched the locket to her heart. The two miniatures of herself and Alexander that he had painted that far-away August day, were tucked inside.

Still she paced.

She glanced toward the horizon and saw the faintest pinkish glow as the moonlight faded and the rays of sun tinged the blue gulf to gold.

She swallowed and stared at the brick walls of the tiny cell. She had to be strong in the face of death.

At least they couldn't take away her hopes, her dreams, her wishes. She closed her eyes, as she imagined:

...the heavy gold compass lay in her palm, filling her with warmth that made her heed neither the wet nor the cold.

She stroked a finger on the ornately carved faceplate of the compass then scanned the horizon again. She raised the spyglass to her eye.

There.

Her heart pounded.

There he was.

But her heart climbed into her throat. A long jagged crack ran down the three-masted schooner's hull from stem to stern. And it listed badly.

Those blasted colonists.

She gripped the compass more tightly then clutched it to her heart.

Seconds ticked by like centuries as the ship limped into the harbor. As it breached the low water mark and began to head toward shore and the docks, she lifted her skirts and raced down the winding iron staircase and out into the wide rolling lawn, then down the street.

At this early hour, fortunately, no one was around to see such unladylike behavior as her churning arms and legs as she raced to the quay.

The scent of fish and tar stung her nose as she clattered onto the weathered dock. Her chest heaved as she finally came to a stop at the very farthest edge of the wooden moorings.

The ship slowly inched its way up to the dock then threw anchor and put down the gang plank.

"Miss, Miss, you can't be coming up here."

She ignored the man's voice.

She plunged up the narrow gangway and onto the wooden deck, its surface stained with God knew what. But she ignored that, too. Her eyes darted left and right.

"Miss," said a voice behind her, "I'm afraid you'll have to leave. I might be forced to walk the plank if I allow a lady aboard."

She spun around, a laugh of pure joy bubbling up within her. She threw her arms around Alexander's neck. "You always joke when you have good news. What is it this time?"

His brown eyes twinkled. "Why, it's that I've returned home to you, of course." He cupped her face gently in his hands and kissed her. He tasted of rum and salt and himself.

He pulled back a fraction and stroked her cheek. "If it wasn't for the compass, I would've never found my way back to you. Never known you were my one and only," he whispered. "But that compass is truly magical."

"I know," she said, and raised up on her tiptoes and kissed him again. "That's why we must guard it with our lives, and pass it down *to our children when the time is right..."*

She opened her eyes. A single tear slipped down her cheek. Dawn. It was time.

Ruby took a jagged breath as if she had been running hard, squeezed her eyes shut then opened them wide. She forced herself to take more lungfuls of air as her heart-beat returned to normal.

"What is it?" Nathan said, reaching for her arm.

She fought down a flutter of residual panic. The compass? Her eyes widened. Edwina had been in jail—about to die. But she had the compass? No, she was imagining she had the compass again, imagining her reunion with Alexander...

Ruby's fingers trembled. "I don't—I don't know. Like a vision. Memory?"

Nathan swallowed. Clenched his jaw. "I've been having...visions...too."

Just then the cab pulled to the curb.

Ruby's fingers trembled and her throat felt raw. "You have?" She looked at Nathan and opened her mouth. But no words came out. How could she tell him about her dreams, or visions, or...whatever they were, *now*? She couldn't risk being that vulnerable. Not now.

But Nathan didn't reply to her question. Simply reached around her to open the cab door. "So this is really it then? You're giving up."

Ruby clenched her jaw. "I'm not giving up. I'm going to the job interview. Sometimes, when you don't find what you're looking for, you need to do something else. Formulate a new theory." She clenched her teeth. She had to get away from here. From him. Go back to Boston and get some perspective.

Why had she allowed him to affect her this much? Her chest tightened. To let him into her life, into her heart, when she'd known all along that it would be a dead end? That she'd lose everything. She forced herself to take a calming breath. No, that was irrational. She hadn't lost anything.

Ruby shifted her purse to her other shoulder. "I have to go. Need to go. My work is done here. I cataloged all the papers. They're being shipped down to Simmons. This position, if I get it, will open up all sorts of doors for me. I need to get on with my life. I can't chase after something that isn't there. We didn't find the order."

"But we still could," Nathan said.

"Nathan, it's a dead end. Sometimes you have to walk away." Her palms felt damp. She looked into his blue eyes. She didn't want to go. Couldn't just leave him here... Yes. Yes, she could. She would leave. She had to leave.

"Walk away." Nathan clenched his jaw. "Like you're doing."

"It's not like that. I just *told* you."

The cab honked. Ruby got inside.

Nathan opened his mouth to say something else but then closed it, his expression shuttered. He rubbed the back of his neck and then raised a hand in farewell.

"Goodbye," she whispered, as the cab sped off. She took a breath. She didn't have time for this. Didn't have time to connect with him, only to have that connection disappear... So she had to be the first to let go. Just like she had with all those other men. This was just like that third-date cliff.

Yes. That was exactly what it was. And now she was ending things before he got a chance to. Safer that way.

NATHAN TAPPED THE pen against the thick manila folder on his desk at the office Monday morning. He startled, as he realized he'd been staring off into space for quite awhile. Ruby had gone. Chosen her career instead of him. No, no. He had no say in her life. Not really. Why did he feel so rejected? Deserted?

He opened the folder and glanced down at the sketches.

Paged through them. God.

He raked a hand through his hair. There were five of them in total. And they were all different.

He turned to the very first one. Edwina.

Nathan remembered the wild, free feeling of his brush loaded with color. The heavy weight of the oils on the fine boarhair bristles of the paintbrush. The sheer joy he'd felt as he'd put color after color and shade after shade onto the thick heavy canvas as he'd painted her portrait.

And, most peculiarly, the way that the textures and colors, and even emotions, had seemed real. Not only real, but...familiar.

He inhaled. Did that mean there actually was something to this past-life stuff Ruby had mentioned?

He shook his head. He didn't want to believe it. He leafed through the other pages one by one.

A tall ship with its snow-white sails unfurled, headed toward Charlottetown harbor. A tiny cabin in the woods with smoke that uncurled from its chimney. Nighttime. Only the soft white glow of the moon as it shone down on a beach, deserted except for the faint trace of two sets of footprints.

He set the last one aside. Cocked his head.

The evidence was literally looking back at him. If you could call it that. It was just a bunch of pictures. Things that he could've, very easily, plucked from not his own memories but from some TV show he'd watched or book he'd read.

Besides, if the whole past-life thing was real, then what was the point if you forgot everything anyway when you were born again?

That familiar tug of longing he felt every time he held a pencil in his hands, welled up within him. He sighed and ran a hand through his hair. But he couldn't push that feeling aside any longer.

It wouldn't just go away if he kept shoving it down. It needed to be acknowledged. It needed to be acted upon. It needed to be validated.

So he turned to his computer and registered for a painting class at Murphy's Community Centre.

THE SHORT, GRAY haired woman smiled at Ruby as she approached the desk. "Hi there. I'm Ruby Zalonski. I have an interview at 9 o'clock this morning for the special collections position."

"Right," she said. "Have a seat."

Ruby sat and tried not to chew on her cuticles. She rummaged around in her purse for a stick of gum instead. She'd left half a pack in here the other day.

Her hand brushed the cool leather journal cover. Almost reflexively, her fingers closed around the small book. It fit comfortably in her hand. As if it was made for her. She'd tucked it in here even though a valuable document like this shouldn't just be thrown in a purse. Yet somehow it brought her reassurance.

She turned the small book over in her hands. A sense of rightness—ownership— swelled within her. No. She tried to shake off the feeling. But it persisted. This couldn't be *her* journal. It was hundreds of years old.

Her heart squeezed.

She glanced at the clock then back at the journal. And risked opening the small volume.

Port-la-Joye   5 Dec. 1775

I've escaped my cell. I pray Alexander has avoided capture on Loyalist ground and brought the Compass as he swore he would do. I do not know if the rose-red moonlight will guide me to our forest rendezvous.

I pray that I am not too late, that Alexander remains unharmed and has stayed well-hidden. That the British, who patrol the fort, Which is perilously near our cabin, do not discover us there.

'Twas I, after all, who laid eyes on him at Cross Keys Tavern that November day. 'Twas I who made him board the ship. If only I'd left him in Charlotte Town, instead of bringing him aboard, then we would've had a chance to be happy together. But now, I fear, we never will. And it is all my own fault.

Ruby frowned. She paged to the end of the journal, but there was nothing there. She flipped back to the beginning.

Charlotte Town   7 Apr. 1774

The British will rue the day they de-

ported my family. Just because the Treaty of Paris was signed eleven years ago doesn't mean that we Acadians agree with our mother country to cede this land to the British. One day, I will strike back. My family is gone. My family heirloom is gone. Bartered away for a freedom that never came. But they will not take me. No. They have taken what is not rightfully theirs. 'Tis a shameful confession but my attempt to regain my heirloom has failed. But I will *get it back.*

"Ruby?" the receptionist said. "Go on back. They're ready for you now."

Ruby startled. Slipped the book back into her purse. Stood. "Uh, sure. Right." She'd figure it all out later. She strode into the meeting room set up for the interview.

The members of the hiring committee stood and shook hands with her.

"Good morning, Ruby. You had a good trip up to the Maritimes? Beautiful country up there," one of the committee members said.

"Yes, I, uh, did." Nathan had said Edwina had been executed in December of 1775...

"So tell us," another committee member said, "what you've been working on and how your researching and cataloging skills fit this position."

...which meant Edwina must have hidden the journal in her cell. Ruby opened her mouth, but nothing came out for a moment. She took a breath. Forced her thoughts back to the question.

"Uh, well, I love research and academics." Ruby paused. "Um, when I was working on cataloging the letters in Dr. O'Neil's collection, I discovered it's important to not only pay attention to what is cataloged, but also to the way things are cataloged."

She shifted in her seat. "I'll defend my doctorate soon. Even though I don't have my Ph.D. yet, I feel that cataloging all of the professor's papers..." She felt a stab of guilt. Nathan had looked so hopeful, so happy, when he'd shown her the journal— "...which he'd donated to this university's archives collection, shows my willingness and abilities in not only cataloging but also in understanding just what..."

Ruby cleared her throat. "Uh, just what goes into big research opportunities." She winced. She could explain things better than this.

But the interviewers just nodded and jotted notes. As the questions continued, Ruby's fists clenched. She had to focus...

"Did you have any more questions for us? Is there anything else you'd like to add?"

"Dr. O'Neil's work is valid and worthy of consideration," she blurted. "And I believe mine is, too." She stood. Straightened her spine. "Because he believed in his work and I believe in my own work. And if you're going to judge me, or my work, based on the hearsay of others in this department, then, well, I believe that's your loss. Because my research speaks for itself. And that should be enough to satisfy anyone." Ruby pushed up her glasses.

The committee members exchanged glances then scribbled something down on their notepads.

Ruby fought a sinking feeling. There went her chance at the job.

All the members of the hiring committee stood up. Shook Ruby's hand again. "Well, Miss Zalonski, that will be all. Thank you for coming in. We'll be in touch."

THAT EVENING AFTER work, Nathan ran a

hand across his face and headed down to his basement studio. He picked up his laptop that lay on the coffee table and absently clicked onto Google. In one corner of the room, he'd propped the almost-complete painting of Edwina.

Ruby's hazel eyes flitted through Nathan's memory. She wasn't from around here, that was sure. Not with a name like...what was it again? Zamboni? No. That was an ice-cleaning machine used for skating rinks. Oh, Zalonski. That was it. What origin was it? It sounded Slavic. Or maybe Russian. Polish? He typed her name into the search box and hit enter.

Hmmm. No Facebook or Twitter account. He scrolled down. His eyes landed on the link to her page from Simmons College.

But he sat back, his finger poised mid-click. Uh-oh. He'd done it again, hadn't he? He shook his head. Thinking about her. Looking her up online... He sighed. This wasn't a good sign.

But he clicked on the link to her CV anyway. And then on her dissertation abstract. As he scanned it, he realized it must have been written long before she'd come up to P.E.I. to sort his dad's papers, because some of her research questions had now been answered.

Archival Studies

In Love & War: A Discourse on Women's Love Letters During The American Revolution

Ruby Zalonski

Dissertation under the direction of Professor Jill Burton

Abstract:

Women's love letters were important documents not only for historical referencing and archival research, but also as a vital means of expression and communication between lovers in times of war.

These letters also gave women voice and outlet for their emotions. An outlet and means that they would not have otherwise been able to have, in polite society, in the latter half of the 18th century. I argue that love letters were an essential and vital means of expression to women in times of war. The numerous love letters collected—in particular, the love letter fragment found by Ruby Zalonski and written to a woman named Edwina Belliveaux—supports this idea. Further postulation holds that there are additional love letters to and from Edwina.

This dissertation also puts forth that Edwina may have been a spy for General George Washington, as evidenced by the cross-reference of the love letter fragment addressed to 'My Darling Edwina' and George Washington's signed order, dated Nov. 23, 1775.

Supporting documents:

(1) love letter fragment, to an 'Edwina,' dated Dec. 2, 1775, given to Ruby Zalonski from an antique book dealer in Boston who found it in an old family bible in their collection

(2) signed orders from Gen. George Washington dated Oct. 15, 1775 and Nov. 23, 1775

(29) love letters from Smithsonian Institute between prominent patriot and his betrothed

(12) love letters from the collection of
a Mrs. H. Robinson, as addressed to
her ancestor while he fought at the
Battle of King's Mountain during
the Revolutionary War

(18) love letters between prominent
Bostonian socialite and her
betrothed in France

Ruby's face swirled through Nathan's head again. She'd come here to do a job, he reminded himself. And that's what had happened. It was simply the facts she'd collected. And now she was gone.

His eyes flicked up to his painting. His brows drew together and he crossed his arms, suddenly cold despite the warm room.

A frisson of longing passed through him and he realized it was because of the painting. He stared at it. Blinked. Looked again.

Nathan froze.

There was something about Edwina's eyes that reminded him of Ruby. Not...directly. But somehow, her eyes helped him to *remember* Ruby. Why was that?

It was as if she was...somehow...inside Ruby or...Ruby was inside her. He shook his head. It didn't make any sense. And yet...it did. Well, they did say the eyes were the windows to the soul...

RUBY RUBBED HER eyes. She forced them wide open and didn't bother to stifle a yawn. She'd been back in Boston a week now. She could continue to look at this tomorrow.

Yet the cramped, faded handwriting kept her reading anyway. She tapped her finger against her chin. What was the connection between the compass and the seal?

She turned another page.

Edwina hadn't written down anything that explained Alexander's coded message about a compass rose in that letter he'd written, either.

Hmmm. A compass was a tool for finding out what direction you were going in. And a compass rose was used on a compass to display the cardinal directions.... Wait a second. *Cardinal directions of the heart...*

There must be some connection. But she was too tired now to think about it. Ruby reached up and switched off the lamp. She'd figure it out tomorrow.

THAT SAME NIGHT, Nathan walked back up the basement stairs and into his bedroom. He flicked on the lamp on the nightstand and remembered his argument with Ruby in the study. She was right. He had been irrational.

He sat down on the dark blue bedspread. Sighed. Had he been naive enough to allow himself to let Ruby in? To entertain the thought that maybe, just maybe, she could've been...special?

No. He shook his head. It went far deeper than that.

She had awakened something within him that he hadn't known existed, before he met her. Yet some part of him—part of who he was, part of what he was—shouted: 'this is it!' But *that* couldn't be.

Could it?

Was she—this feeling—the whole reason he'd always felt so empty inside with other women? Always wanted to put on the brakes, say no, end things, break up, cut off engagements?

Because of this tiny piece of dissatisfaction that gnawed at him, that wouldn't allow him to fully give his heart wholly to anyone. No matter how much he'd want to, no matter how much the other women had loved him. He just couldn't return their love. To any of them.

Any of them before now, that is?

He swallowed, his throat suddenly dry.

But he didn't, couldn't, have feelings for Ruby. He'd only just met her, for Chrissakes.

This...this thing that he couldn't even begin to describe. And this thing that had made him push her away.

He sat up. Sudden anger coursed through him. If that were true, if she was more than special to him, and if there was something—just maybe—to that reincarnation thing, then why hadn't they been able to overcome their differences and be together?

He shoved those thoughts aside and the anger faded. He had no one to blame but himself. What was he going to do? Dad's hearing was tomorrow. Ruby wasn't here. She couldn't add credibility to the hearing on his dad's behalf.

He rolled over onto his back. Sighed. Then folded his arms over his bare chest and, after what seemed like hours, finally fell asleep.

His hands, though slippery with sweat,

nonetheless gripped the reins with the tightness and conviction of a condemned criminal, though his travel and duties were not that of any sort of prisoner. His heart pounded. He was still a wanted man, down in the 13 colonies. But was he safe up here?

No matter. If endangering his own life would bring him even one step closer to his Edwina, it would be worth it. He didn't care if he had to fight off the entire British navy to get her back.

He saw the pink light of dawn filter through the pine trees near Fort Amherst. And the prison.

Edwina.

His heart squeezed and his fingers clutched the box to his chest. He'd returned to the island with it safely. Now he just had to get to her. Had to rescue her. Save her from a fate she didn't deserve. She couldn't die. She was only trying to get back what was rightfully hers. The compass.

Because when he'd been accosted by his brother, there in Boston, he'd had to hand over the seal. He'd managed to keep the compass. But only just. Simply because the Americans believed he only carried an empty box.

The horse's hooves churned up sand on the moonlit beach. He kept the cloak's hood drawn up around his face. He'd come this far. He clutched the box tighter. He saw the lights of Fort Amherst in the distance. If he delivered it to her there then she'd be safe. And they could be together again. At last.

But first he would see if, perchance, Edwina had somehow gotten away from her captors and was about to meet him at their rendezvous. On their six-day journey together from Charlotte Town to Boston, the cabin was the place that he and Edwina had promised they'd meet, if trouble arose.

He'd managed to smuggle a coded letter to Molly at the tavern, in case Edwina was able to make her way there and ask for him.

The brim of his tricorn hat slipped low over his eyes with the frenzied gallop across the sand and into an open moonlit meadow full of wild roses. Flecks of sweat from the stallion, coupled with the rhythmic pounding of its hooves, did nothing to still the pounding of his own heart as he remembered that November night aboard the ship bound for Boston...

"I've made a mistake. I never should have involved you in this raid. I'm sorry," she said to him. Her green eyes studied him with uncertainty.

"I should not have known one such as yourself if you hadn't. Regret nothing." He stroked a finger down the satiny contour of her cheek. His skin wiped away the trail of moisture that had accumulated there.

"We'll be together. Somehow. When all of this is over," he whispered. "When we first met that day in August, I had no idea—and neither did you—of what would happen. No one did."

He clenched the fingers of his free hand together into a fist. "You know I cannot stay away from you. I love you."

The cabin lights were lit. His heart leapt. She was there.

His thoughts flitted back to that night in the moonlight, the love in her large green eyes. The way she'd tasted when he'd kissed her.

The scent of wild roses that clung to her skin as they'd lain on the beach together. The roar of the surf at least as loud as the blood pounding in his veins each time he looked at her.

And now, if he didn't get to her in time, she was going to be executed for being a traitor. All because she'd wanted her compass back, and stolen the seal, instead.

He squeezed his hands into fists. She didn't deserve to be treated like that. It didn't make her a traitor. The Crown, in fact, had been a traitor to her and her family when *they'd deported her loved ones despite their payment in solid gold.*

The light in the cabin flickered. He pulled the reins up short and dismounted. He led the bay stallion over to the low-hanging branch of a chestnut tree, its branches mere silhouettes in the light of the waning moon.

His footsteps light and anticipatory, her name on his lips, he stepped into the cabin. "My love," he whispered.

"Good evening. I trust you had a pleasant ride." The muzzle of a musket instead of his lady's open arms, greeted him. And that uniform—it could be none other than a British officer's.

"Now hand over your precious cargo. Stolen property of the Crown."

When he didn't move, the officer nudged him with the weapon. "The seal," he hissed. "I know you have it."

"I swear to you, I do not."

"Lying Patriot." The officer spat. "For that, you shall die."

Nathan awoke with a start. His heart pounded and his hands clenched so tightly into fists that his fingers began to cramp. He took a deep breath then let it out slowly.

But his heart still pounded.

It was just a dream. But it felt so real.

He sat up. Dreams always felt real to him. Ever since he'd had that nightmare as a 7-year-old. Where people in funny hats with strange accents were trying to stab him.

He shuddered at the memory.

Dreams felt especially real when he was under stress.

All right. Breathe in. He felt his shoulders relax, his heart rate drop. Breathe out. He continued to breathe slowly through his nose.

Just a dream.

That was all. No, no it wasn't. Was it? He rolled to the side of his bed. Now, he couldn't sleep.

He got out of bed to splash some water on his face and almost tripped over the trash can on his way to the bathroom. He swore and went into the bathroom. The dim light from the streetlights outside made shadows jump out.

Nathan scraped a hand across his unshaven cheeks. He tossed the towel onto the faux-marble countertop but forgot to dry off his face.

He returned to his bedroom and propped himself up against the blond wood headboard. Then he brought his knees up to his bare chest.

He glanced at the clock. 1:45 a.m.

He couldn't deny it any more. These dreams...there was something to them. Something unfinished—restless—in his soul, that was trying to communicate to his consciousness. And it all started with Ruby. And that journal. He couldn't rationalize this away any more. He could still smell the wood smoke. Taste the memory of her kiss. Feel the weight of that gold object... Gold object? The compass. He held his breath. Let it out. Yes... The compass, as crazy as it sounded, *was* real.

He blinked. Took a breath. Why did he care?

His thoughts went back to Ruby's Simmons College webpage. It wasn't his own secrets she'd posted online. It was one of the love letters from Alexander to Edwina, that she'd put up, along with her CV.

He shook himself. He stood up and began pacing. *He* wasn't the one who'd written the letter. Goose bumps broke out on his skin.

Was he?

Damn it. He was in love with Ruby. He exhaled and stared out the window at the pouring rain. He crossed his arms. He'd told her everything. Completely let her in.

He rubbed his temples. He'd never felt

like this before. Hoping... No, not hoping. Knowing. Beyond the shadow of a doubt. That he was right for her. And that she was right for him.

But did she feel it too? Or was this just lust and loneliness talking?

He shivered.

The rain fell harder. It pounded on the roof. Nathan's thoughts drifted back to his last conversation with Ruby.

Growing up, he used to have these vivid dreams in which he was wearing clothing from different eras and speaking in funny ways. He used to tell his mom about them but as time had gone on, they'd come less and less, until finally, they'd stopped.

But that was before a few weeks ago. Those dreams had been so vivid, felt so...real...that he'd almost sworn he had actually been there. Back in the 1700s. Living someone else's life...someone else's life that felt much like his own.

But that wasn't possible. Everything ended after you died. Didn't it? He picked up the glass of water on his nightstand and his thoughts shifted back to Ruby. Why did he think she was so different from all the other women he'd known?

What if this was just his ego telling him

this time things were different? This time she was The One? This time—he drained the glass's contents—this time she'd left.

He got back in bed and fell into a deep, dreamless sleep.

RUBY SAT UP all at once. The digital readout on her alarm clock said 1:45 a.m.

She blinked and fumbled with the bed-spread then disentangled herself. She rolled over. Half-remembered images tumbled through her mind. No, not just images. She sat up. Her nightgown clung to her. Memories. Intense memories. She blushed in the dark.

She brought a hand up to her throat and felt her pulse pound beneath her fingertips.

Oh... Moonlight. His lips, warm and tender, and hers, seeking and urgent. Their embrace, a promise made to be broken. The sharp sea spray and the taste of salt on his kiss.

Her fingers clutched the solid oak ship's railing. Her heart, heavy as lead, as she watched the shoreline fade into the distance.

The safe security of his arms around

her as they slid to the sand. Her pressing against the firm solidity of his chest, heat spreading through her.

The rough scrape of his stubble against her fingertips. She cradled his face between her hands. A deep knowingness and rightness welled within her. As if he was made for her, and she, for him. As if she could tell him her every secret, reveal every flaw, and still be adored. Honored. Beloved.

She'd tried to save him. Tried...and failed.

Ruby pressed a hand to her heart. She turned the dream memories over in her mind as the image of a compass, reflecting the moonlight, came to her consciousness.

Ruby took a ragged breath and finally felt her hammering heart slow to a more normal rhythm.

She took another breath and reached for the glass of water on her bedside table. She drained the contents. Then she swung her legs over the edge of the bed and got up. She walked to the window. Looked out.

She didn't even realize she was looking for the moon until she saw it, framed between the branches of a chestnut tree in the yard outside.

She blinked.

There was no chestnut tree in the yard. She took a step back. She shut the blinds with a snap, microwaved herself some hot milk and then crawled back into bed.

But all she could think about was the way Nathan's blue eyes had pierced her as she'd said goodbye to him. How words had stuck in her throat as she'd longed to say more.

Finally she fell back into sleep.

The next time Ruby opened her eyes, sunlight streamed through the thick slats of the blinds, which created a striped pattern across her pale green duvet.

She sat up. Memories of last night faded into the background. She bit her lip and then got up out of bed. Made herself some breakfast and then began unpacking her carry-on, just as the phone rang.

"Hello?" She didn't recognize the caller ID.

"Good morning, Ruby. This is the dean's office calling. You've been offered the position."

NATHAN'S ALARM WENT off at 7 a.m. He yawned, stretched, got out of bed and rummaged around for a T-shirt. He picked up the one from last night that he'd flung next to the clothes hamper. He pulled it on. Clean enough.

Then he put on a pair of pants and ambled into the kitchen. Making breakfast would kill some time until it was a decent hour for him to go over there and take another stab at looking for the order.

He switched on the coffee pot. Plopped a slice of bread into the toaster.

He rummaged in the fridge and poured himself some orange juice. The toast popped up out of the toaster and he reached for a butter knife to load the golden brown slice with a generous slathering of gooseberry jam. His favorite.

The coffee pot began percolating, so he reached for a mug from the dishwasher he'd forgotten to empty yesterday.

He poured himself a cup of coffee, black, and went to the table to sit and eat.

But he burned his tongue on the coffee and discovered that the underside of the toast had burnt.

He muttered under his breath. Just when he felt he'd started to figure things out, it all shifted and this was what happened. Stubbed toes. Burnt toast. And, he grimaced, bitter coffee grounds.

He dumped the coffee out in the sink

and tossed the partially eaten toast into the compost bin. Well, he glanced at the clock, at least now he could reasonably go over and talk to Ruby.

No, he remembered. He couldn't. She was gone. Suddenly he wasn't hungry.

Damn it. He shoved back his chair. Where was all of this coming from? Before she came along, his life had been just fine.

He clenched his jaw. That was irrational. It wasn't *her* fault.

Shit. He really did have feelings for her, didn't he? He threw a sideways glance out the window in the direction of downtown.

No. He ground his teeth. He couldn't have feelings for her. Not now. When it was too late.

Chapter Seven

*I*NSTEAD OF THE relief and happiness Ruby expected to feel, she bit her lip and gripped the phone tighter. "I—" She swallowed. Finished unpacking her small carry-on case and zipped it shut. But the zipper stuck. It caught on a piece of crumpled paper.

She pulled it out.

A photocopy of the second of Washington's orders. Ruby sighed and put it on the dresser. She had to find it *now*?

She set that aside and looked down again at the letter she'd found only yesterday tucked between the journal's pages. The connection between the compass and Edwina and Alexander.

Port-la-Joye   2 Dec. 1775

Darling Alexander,
It has Lately come to my attention—

and my heart—just how much the compass has its own set of Powers. If some mishap should befall us, I have devised a plan of safekeeping for the Compass. Mistress McDuff knows of it.

When I touched its surface, a thousand feelings and memories touched not only my mind but also my heart. I knew in an instant that your and my meeting that moonlit August night 'twas no accident.

I await Word of my Fate this day. I had heard of your narrow escape of imprisonment for desertion from sailors' talk on my shipboard journey northward, and prayed for Word from you. How happy I am to have received your encoded missive even in this wretched cell. Once I decoded the letter, it Pained me to read your words. How you believed that I betrayed your trust in choosing to not reveal my spying to you while we were aboard ship to Boston.

I am gladder still of your foresight, upon hearing of W's Order for my forced exit of Boston, in securing the Seal and Compass. But it gladdens me most of all to know you chose to forgive me for withholding my spying from you, in those last few lines of secret post-script.

Even if your brother implored you to give up the Seal at musket-point for the value in silver Coinage it would fetch him, I applaud your Brave heart in holding fast to your convictions and not letting the Compass fall into the Wrong hands. Your Loyalty and Love in volunteering to bring it back to the island, and risking your own life to do so, fills me with such admiration and gratitude.

Oh how I long to feel those hands of yours along my blushing cheeks. But I trust that with Good faith I shall be in your arms once more, before the new moon reaches its zenith.

Always your True Love,
Edwina

"I'll accept the position," Ruby heard herself say even as she glanced back at the letter. Then she found herself reach for the copy of the order.

"Well, Ruby, that's great."

She fiddled with the pencil in her hand.

Found herself counting lines and spaces. She sank her teeth into her bottom lip. She'd painted Nathan in black and white, assumed he was just like what everyone said about him, when the reality was...She cocked her head.

Ruby put the order back down on the dresser. She had to find a way to accept him for who he was, not just assume he was one way or the other. She had to forgive him his faults and focus on his good qualities. She glanced down at the order again. Was the rest of the message there? And if it was, would it help her make up with Nathan?

She felt her heart expand and a blush color her cheeks as soft and gentle warmth spread through her. Try and deny it though she might, she did care about him.

She picked up the page from the dresser.

Memories washed over her. Him giving the change to the homeless man in the rain. Him taking the time to help her with the research—and taking time away from his own job to do it. The look of...tenderness...in his blue eyes as he watched her in the alcove.

No, Nathan wasn't the bad guy she'd mistaken him for. But would he even care if the rest of the message was deciphered?

"We'll get all the paperwork together and then set up a time for you to come and sign it."

"Okay," she murmured into the phone.

"We'll be in touch."

"Great," Ruby said, and ended the call. She reached for the pad of paper on her dresser to scribble the rest of the decoded message from the second order.

Where good sirs gather
Under the sign of the Keys

Her heart pounded. Did that mean Cross Keys Condos was involved in this riddle? She chewed on the end of the pencil. Her phone buzzed again. Dr. Burton.

"Hi," Ruby said, and heard the rustle of papers on Dr. Burton's end of the line.

"Congratulations, Ruby! You got the job."

"Thanks. That was a quick decision on their part." Ruby blurted.

"The thing is," Dr. Burton said, "what with your corresponding with Dr. O'Neil, and his research being investigated, well, the hiring committee decided to push things along so word doesn't spread too far into the academic community."

"Oh." Ruby said. "Right. That makes sense."

"So. Are you going in over the next few days to sign the paperwork and make it official before your dissertation defense?"

"Not quite. There's somewhere I have to go, first."

"Oh?"

"Prince Edward Island. I have to...wrap up my research there." Find out where this riddle led.

Dr. Burton sighed. "That's why I called." Ruby could imagine her advisor's perfectly plucked brows drawing together in a frown. "Your funding for the love letter research grant's been cut."

Ruby sank onto the bed. "What?" She chewed on a cuticle. "How is that even possible?"

"Well, you remember when they built the new stadium awhile back? Turns out they went over-budget. So they're having to reallocate funds from other departments to cover the costs."

Ruby's stomach knotted. She was so close to figuring all of this out. Now that she had Edwina's journal, and figured out what the rest of the riddle was, she couldn't just walk away. Nathan's face rose in her mind.

She was going to be true to herself, to her own feelings, her own heart.

"Ruby? I know what that silence means. You're thinking. What are you thinking?"

Ruby sighed. "I have to go back up there. I need to. Not just for my research, but for... Well, I just do."

"But there's no more money. You can't."

Ruby pushed up her glasses. She logged onto her online bank account. Only $400 left in her savings account now. Well, if it used up the last of her savings, it would be worth it. She needed to talk to Nathan. Needed to help him. Because he was right. A promise to help was a promise.

She felt a strength surge through her. She had to be willing to trust her own feelings, her own emotions and her own mind, in order to risk making that real connection with him. The one she craved. The one she deserved. And the one that she hoped she hadn't completely destroyed.

NATHAN SHRUGGED INTO his dark blue suit

jacket and adjusted his tie. He stepped out of his car at the UPEI campus and headed into the meeting room.

He tucked the folder under his arm and went up the stairs to meet his lawyer, who was standing outside the door of the meeting room.

"Right on time, Nathan," she said. "Let's do this."

Nathan nodded. Tightened his jaw.

"We'll do the best we can. I know you've tried your hardest to find the order. And I have all the evidence you could gather, right here with me." She patted a fat leather briefcase.

Nathan gave her a tight smile. It was time to get this done and over with. "I have to speak on Dad's behalf, even though we never found anything. Even though I looked everywhere." He adjusted his cufflinks then held the door open for her.

"Welcome, everyone." The chair for the committee on academic misconduct cleared his throat as the door swung shut silently behind Nathan.

The man continued. "We're here to discuss the series of allegations made against Dr. Gordon O'Neil's research."

Nathan sat.

"Shall we begin?"

After awhile, Nathan glanced at the clock on the wall. Fifty minutes had passed. He shifted in the hard oak chair. Cleared his throat.

"And now, the committee will recommend to the university senate that Dr. Gordon O'Neil's title of emeritus will be removed, effective immediately." The committee chairman surveyed the room. "Does anyone have any final remarks?" He adjusted his half-glasses.

"Yes," Nathan said. "I'd like to go on record as saying that the credit for working to clear my father's name, goes in part to Ruby Zalonski."

The chairman nodded. "Then—"

But suddenly the door opened. Nathan swivelled in his seat.

Ruby stood in the doorway.

"THAT SECOND SIGNED order from General Washington. That's why I came back." Ruby paused to take a deep breath as she stood on the threshold of the meeting room.

It didn't matter what Nathan or anyone else thought. Or said. Or even did. What she had to do was tell him what she knew.

She owed it to Edwina. And Dr. O'Neil. So she continued.

"Your famous historical figure, Edwina Belliveaux?" Ruby stepped fully into the room. "Washington knew she was a spy. But what he didn't know was *why*. But I do. The charges against Dr. O'Neil should be dropped. Edwina led the raid on Charlottetown. I have the proof right here, if that's what you're looking for." She held up an antique letter and the journal.

Ruby saw Nathan's knuckles turn white as he gripped the arms of his chair. She moved to stand beside him then raised her voice to address everyone in the room. "Washington knew she was a turncoat. She was helping him. But what he didn't know was why she was actually loyal to her *own* people. The Acadians. Not the British. That's why she'd—"

The dean looked at Ruby. "Edwina Belliveaux did not do all those things. She was an upstanding citizen. She told the Americans to leave the seal alone. She—"

"She was a spy, sir. Not a privateer. Not a saint. But a spy."

The dean opened his mouth to protest.

"Dr. O'Neil seemed to think she was." Ruby waved the article she held in her left hand. "That's what his own journal says. And I have the original journal of Edwina

Belliveaux's here, too."

"It will, of course, have to be authenticated," the dean said.

"Yes," Ruby straightened her shoulders. Pushed up her glasses. "It will. But I assure you, you will find it to be one hundred percent real. Edwina was responsible for the schooners coming up to P.E.I. And she was responsible for the raid on Charlottetown. And she was responsible for kidnapping not only Callbeck and Wright but also a man named Alexander McEachern."

"WHO?" BUT ALL the blood had drained from Nathan's face. Alexander. *He* was Alexander. And she—Nathan caught his breath—was Edwina.

"It sounds like you already know him." Ruby tapped a foot on the polished floorboards, and Nathan noticed her toenail polish, underneath the peep-toes of her pumps, was that same pale pink he'd seen the first time he'd met her.

Nathan closed his eyes but couldn't shut out Ruby's hazel ones. He opened his eyes and looked down at the page in her hand.

"That's why she came up to Charlotte-town with Captain Selman and Captain Broughton in the first place."

"But how do you *know* this?" the dean demanded.

Ruby held up the cracked leather-bound volume. Tiny pieces of leather flaked off its gold-embossed cover and fell onto the floor.

Nathan reached a hand out and stroked a fingertip along the journal's surface and addressed the dean. "I found that at Fort Amherst."

"Also known as Port-la-Joye—that's what Edwina called it in her journal," Ruby added. "That's where she was executed."

The dean held up his hands. "This case is on hold. Based on examination of the new evidence presented today, in light of the forgery charges, your lawyers will be notified regarding further proceedings."

Everyone filed out of the room.

Beside him, Nathan heard his lawyer breathe a sigh of relief as they stepped out of the building and into the sunshine.

"Thank you, Ruby," she said. "I'll let you both know when things re-convene. We'll be in touch," she said to Nathan, and gave him a maternal smile. "In the meantime, it looks like you two have some things to discuss." The lawyer winked, waved and headed to her Mercedes.

Nathan turned to Ruby. He swallowed and angled his head to look at her. "You know who Edwina hoped would came back for her." It wasn't a question.

In the near-empty parking lot, Nathan realized, he and Ruby stood only inches apart. "Yes," she breathed. "Alexander."

Nathan's gaze bored into hers. "And why did *you* come back, Ruby?"

His voice trailed to a whisper, and he saw her eyes dart from his gaze to the pavement and back up again.

His breath stirred a stray curl that had come loose from the messy ponytail she seemed to always have her hair done up in.

He wondered how she'd react if he reached up and slid that pencil out from its secure place in her thick brunette waves and buried his fingers in her silky strands.

He could feel the soft warmth of her breath on his cheek. Saw the questioning look in her hazel eyes. He slowly reached up and tucked the stray curl behind her ear. He saw her eyelids flutter, and a faint pink color her cheeks. Held his breath. He turned his palm so that his fingers now brushed the side of her face, and watched her lips part as he slowly, gently, stroked the pad of his thumb across her cheek-bone.

He leaned closer. The scent of wild roses filled his head. He saw the pulse jump in her throat and felt her body stiffen, saw her lips tremble.

"I would never hurt you," he whispered.

"I know," she whispered back, as a tear slid down her cheek. "But I've accepted that job. I start Monday."

His gut tightened and he dropped his hand from her face. "Oh." He took a step back. Fiddled with the button on his suit jacket. He buttoned it, glad for something to distract himself from the clench of anxiety that had suddenly formed in his chest. She'd deserted him. Just like she had before. Suddenly he couldn't breathe.

But he forced his lungs to expand. So that was it, was it? She hadn't really come back because of him, at all. Only to do her duty. For her career. He frowned.

Ruby must have seen the look in his eyes because she crossed her arms then said, "Nathan. I don't want to fight with you. Does it matter?"

"It does to me."

"Fine. I'm sorry. Is that what you want? An apology?"

Nathan didn't reply. Just clenched his jaw.

Ruby held out a lined sheet torn from her yellow legal pad. "This is the other half of the clue. From the second order. I found a copy in Boston that I'd printed out. '*Good Sirs gather/under the sign of the Keys*'"

"You—" Nathan swallowed hard, "—deserted me." He ignored the piece of paper. "You expect me to just jump right back in and help you with this now that you've figured it out?" He crossed his arms. "Now that you've gone to your interview? Now that you've just happened to come in and miraculously produce evidence that may save my dad's reputation? That may lead to the compass? Well, no thank you. I'm not going to help you. Go find it yourself if you want it so badly. You obviously don't care about anything but how it'll look on your academic record."

Ruby's hands tightened into fists. "Fine. Looks like I won't be needing this anymore, either." Ruby shoved the small leather-bound book at Nathan, who automatically reached out to prevent the book from falling. But as he did so, their fingers collided and the book fell onto the ground.

Ruby let out a cry of dismay and knelt

to pick up the book. But as she reached out and picked it back up, she froze. Raised her eyes up to Nathan's. "Do you see what I see?"

Nathan crouched down beside Ruby and angled his head. He could see the pulse flutter at her throat.

She swallowed and pointed to the pressed-together pages. On the flat surface created by the pages being pressed together, were faint ink markings.

"It's a sketch of a wild rose. And a compass."

Chapter Eight

LATER THAT SAME evening, Nathan raked a hand through his hair. His thoughts kept turning round and round about what Ruby had done. *She came back,* a voice in his head whispered.

Her hazel eyes flashed through his mind as he took a handful of salt and vinegar Covered Bridge chips from the bag on the counter after his art class. A smile that Nathan couldn't quash rested on his lips as he spotted his sketchpad and pencils in a tote bag slung over a kitchen chair.

He pulled the instructor's business card out of his pocket. It was just like P.E.I. that she'd been Dad's neighbor. He smiled.

Even better was that the instructor had mentioned that their company was looking for a new intern, since theirs had just graduated. She didn't seem to mind that Nathan was older than the average student.

Nathan shook his head. He wouldn't

have had this opportunity to actually pursue his passion if it hadn't been for that sketch....

But the thought of his drawing made him think of Ruby. Why was he always feeling this sadness whenever he was around her? It was as if the sadness came from—he squinted and took another chip— a memory associated with her.

He frowned and took another chip. Flipped on a comedy show and tried to forget about it. But it was only when the presenter had told his fourth joke that Nathan realized he couldn't forget about it at all.

He took another chip and turned off the TV. Might as well go to bed. But just as he entered his bedroom, his phone rang.

"Nathan, sorry to bother you this late at night. But I've just gotten a call from the committee chair," the lawyer said. "Seems that someone on the committee wasn't satisfied with how things turned out today. One of the members still insists your dad's findings are all bunk. Even with the new evidence. So they've all stayed late and pushed through a vote. And, well, your dad's research, along with all his work, has been declared completely invalid."

Nathan caught his breath. Sank onto

the edge of his bed. "But—but the original letter? The journal?" He blinked, his throat tight. "None of it was good enough?"

"No."

"But—"

"I know, Nathan. I'm sorry. We tried."

Nathan jumped up and started to pace. "That's not good enough." He resisted the urge to put his fist through the wall. "All that time." He raked his hands through his hair. "All that energy." He ground his teeth. "All that *work*. That I did. That Ruby did. That my d—dad did..." His throat tightened. "That can't be the end of things." He narrowed his eyes. "That won't be the end of things. I'll see to it. Justice has to be served. The wrongs have to be righted. I'm going to *find* that order. Find the seal, if it's still out there. And find the compass. Put it all to rights." Nathan said, and ended the call. Tossed the phone onto the nightstand. His mind flicked back to Ruby.

What if she disappeared on him? And what if that was entirely his fault? His pulse sped up. What if he couldn't prevent her from leaving? His mouth had gone dry. What if he couldn't prevent her from being hurt, from being forever taken away from him?

He stood and rubbed his temples. He was getting carried away. He'd take a hot shower. Relax. Then he'd finally maybe be able to fall asleep tonight without disturbing dreams.

After he finished his shower, he tucked a blue paisley-print towel around his waist then towel-dried his hair.

On impulse, Nathan padded barefoot down the basement stairs. Gave a frustrated sigh. He'd lost his cool—again. Acted completely irrationally there in the parking lot. He flicked on the light.

He wandered over to the painting, which he'd now completed. He'd looked at the picture a thousand times before. He cocked his head.

Edwina's honey-blonde hair was windblown, though she stood inside a room next to a window that was firmly shut.

In one hand, she held a half-open rosebud, its petals a swirl of blood-red and white. Her other hand was splayed against the slippery peacock-blue silk of her ruffled gown with ruched stomacher and square neckline.

Nathan followed Edwina's gaze out the window to a moonlit, storm-tossed ship half-visible through the lacy curtain that fluttered at the six-pane window.

And though Nathan had captured her smiling, it was her eyes—filled with reflections of guilt and sadness—that made his heart squeeze.

Just then, the doorbell rang.

RUBY STOOD ON Nathan's doorstep. The doorbell glowed, a small amber dot against the dark paint of the doorframe. She heard the soft chirps of crickets in Charlotte-town's East Royalty subdivision.

Ruby shifted her weight from one foot to the other and studied the way the light caught the leaded panes of frosted glass set into the panelled door. Maybe she should have waited till morning.

But this was important. She knew he'd want to know that his dad had been on the right track all along, that there *was* a connection between the compass and the Great Seal.

She pressed her finger against the doorbell again and a series of chimes rang out in the stillness.

Crickets chirped.

A car went by.

And no one answered the door.

Well, she'd tried. She hiked her purse

up onto her shoulder and started to turn away from the door when it opened.

In the half-light from the hallway, Ruby swallowed. Nathan's face was partially in shadow and the scent of Irish Spring soap drifted to her. He wore only a terrycloth towel wrapped around his waist.

Their eyes met.

He didn't say anything. Neither did she.

She didn't move, and her throat tightened. She could see a single water droplet fall from his damp hair and slide down his neck.

It landed on his bare shoulder. Ruby blinked, her heart pounded, her breath caught. She watched as the drop slid over his collarbone, his skin soft and smooth in the golden light.

But as the water drop slid down onto the smooth, flat plane of his chest, Ruby gasped. She moved forward. Closed the space between them. "You're hurt," she said. The wound puckered angry and red at the midpoint of his chest.

The cabin walls spun around her. He was bleeding. She had to stop the bleeding. He was bleeding so much. She bit her bottom lip so hard she tasted the salty sharp tang of her own blood. Better hers than his.

She pressed her already-soaked handkerchief more firmly to his chest but it only grew darker with his blood. The delicate edging of lace she'd spent hours stitching onto the soft white cotton, now bright red.

Her heart pounded and she clenched her jaw. He would not die. He could not. She fought back a sob but the tears fell anyway, and mingled with the scent of gunpowder, pine and wood smoke. She pressed his cold fingers to her warm cheek.

The tromp of boots on the threshold told her she'd come too late. For both of them.

Her fingers grazed his bare skin, warm to her touch. She heard his intake of breath. She looked up at him, her gaze caught and held there by the depths of his blue eyes. Slowly, ever so slowly, his gaze still locked on hers, he inclined his head toward her.

Her eyes widened even as his briefly closed. He reached up and placed his warm, strong fingers around hers. She felt herself lean forward. She tilted her head up.

"It's not..." Nathan whispered.

She could feel his heart beating under her palm. His skin, not ragged, not torn. But smooth. Soft. Whole. Underneath her fingertips. Her fingers trembled and her lips parted. "Oh God," she murmured, blinked. Her heartbeat sped up.

His lips were only millimeters from hers...

But the honk of a horn, accompanied by catcalls, as a car passed on the street behind them, shattered the silence. Nathan startled and jerked his head back.

"That's not," he opened his eyes, "a wound." He cleared his throat. "That's a birthmark."

"But—" She looked again at the place and blinked. It wasn't swollen or puckered. She grazed her fingertips across it, which caused goose bumps on his damp skin.

"Oh," she said. She dropped her hand from his chest and wrapped her arms around herself.

Nathan shifted his weight. Stepped away from her. "Is everything all right? I was about to go to bed."

"I, uh, sorry. I know it's late. But I couldn't sleep if I didn't come and apologize. I'm sorry. And," she cleared her throat and stepped into the foyer. "I wanted to explain more about what I discovered. I found a letter from Edwina to Alexander about the Great Seal and the compass." She paused. Held Nathan's gaze. "I also deciphered the other order. Then put both halves of the clue together. But I don't know what the riddle means and..." She bit her lip. "I need your help."

Nathan didn't move for a moment. She could feel him look at her, study her, from the semi-darkness of the foyer.

She shifted her weight. Wet her lips.

He let out a breath, and flicked on the overhead light. "I got a call earlier tonight from my lawyer. All my dad's findings, all his research, all his work, was declared invalid. Every. Last. Thing." Nathan ground his teeth. "The journal and the antique letter weren't enough." Nathan's jaw clenched. "So I told her we'd figure it all out. So what's the whole clue again, now, from the orders?"

Ruby read it aloud: *"'Hearts of ink/Sealed in highest wooden frame/where good Sirs gather/under the sign of the Keys'"*

Nathan tapped a finger against the wall. "Let me get dressed. Have a seat in the living room."

Ruby sank onto the black leather couch and waited for Nathan to come back.

"So, *hearts of ink*," Nathan said, after he returned. "Ink could be tattoos. But I doubt it was meant in that way in the 1700s."

"Hmmm...what do you do with ink? You can draw with it. Write with it," Ruby said. "Write…. Wait a minute. Hearts of ink. Hearts of writing…" She paused. "Could it be something about hearts? A story or a letter or a—"

"A poem." Nathan said. "*The Fair Isle Lovers*. Why didn't I see that before? It contains that legend about the compass of true love. And all these clues have been pointing to the compass, in one way or another, all along." Nathan nodded. "It's about that poem."

Ruby shot him an exasperated look. "But what about the rest? I was thinking 'sealed' could be a reference to the seal itself. Or it could mean literally sealed up."

"Well, we don't have the seal. So we'll have to assume it means something else."

"Okay. So how about the next line? *In highest wooden frame*…What has wooden frames?" Ruby glanced at Nathan.

"Lots of things. Doors, windows. Scaffolds. Houses…" he said.

"Houses. Doors. Windows. I think it could be a house," she said.

"Yeah, but which one?" Nathan asked.

"That doesn't mean—Oh." Ruby paused. "*Highest* frame. On a top floor, maybe? What houses had high floors in 1700s Charlottetown?"

"Well, none of them, really," Nathan

said. "They were all just log cabins basically. The only place with multiple stories was...the tavern. Cross Keys Condos used to be Cross Keys Tavern. That's why they kept the name 'cross keys.'"

Ruby grinned at him. "*Under the sign of the keys.* That makes perfect sense. And also fits with 'where good sirs gather.' But what about a wooden frame?"

"Well, I guess we'll just have to check all the windows and doors on the fourth floor. First thing tomorrow morning," Nathan said.

A pause.

Ruby got up off the couch. "Okay, well, um, thanks. I'll just...let you get to bed, then." She tucked a strand of hair behind her ear and headed for the front door.

Nathan cleared his throat. "Right." He followed her to the entryway. "Have a good night, then, Ruby." He closed the door behind her.

RUBY'S MIND WAS still reeling as she got into her bed. She kept seeing the expression on Nathan's face as she'd touched him in the foyer. She rolled over onto her side.

Her stomach tightened. And the *way* she'd touched him. What she'd seen as her fingers had brushed his skin...

Finally, her eyelids fluttered closed and she fell asleep.

Branches and brambles snagged at her long skirts as she stumbled through the darkness. The day was lost. But she was free from the prison and the night might still have hope. That only made her heart pound faster as she continued to run. She was almost there. Almost to him. Alexander.

Her breath came in ragged gasps as she made her way to the tiny pin-prink of light she could see in the distance. Their cabin rendezvous. Where everything was safe and they were together. Warm. Happy.

Tree branches scraped against her skin as she continued to run, the only light coming from the sliver of red harvest moon that scrabbled between clouds in the December darkness. She shivered and watched the ice crystals form in the air as she breathed his name.

Her lungs burned. She was almost there. She had to make it. She would make it. She put on a final burst of speed.

As she approached the clearing, her body sagged with relief. No redcoats. No glint of muskets in the moonlight.

She slowed. Finally came to a halt in front of the rough hand-hewn cabin door. She cocked her head.

She could see the glow of the lamp in the window. She opened the door.

Goose bumps broke out on her skin.

She stepped over the threshold that she had, for so many years, imagined her true love would carry her across on their wedding day.

The room was warm; she shivered. The scent of roasted meat lingered in the air. She turned around and shut the door behind her then rubbed her arms to ward off the chill.

As her eyes adjusted to the soft firelight, she glanced at the hearth.

Then she fell to her knees and pulled out her handkerchief. All the breath left her lungs. She looked down at his face, at the blood on the lace at his throat. Bright crimson seeped through the snowy white fabric. She pressed her handkerchief futilely to his wound.

"No. No, no, no."

She stroked a hand down his cheek. Her own hand still held the letter he'd written her. His skin, cold. She swallowed. Saw the governor's puzzle box and a letter clutched in his unmoving hand.

He was dead. And she was too late.

They'd killed him. Her hands tightened into fists. They'd pay for this. But not before she hid the box, with the compass secreted inside. No one would get that. She'd see to it.

"Alexander," she whispered, before she buried her face in his velvet jacket and sobbed.

Ruby's eyes flew open. Her heart pounded. Alexander was gone. She shivered in the predawn darkness. Gone.

Alexander?

That was no dream. The colors were too vivid. The smells were too strong.

Alexander.

She wiped a tear from her eye and felt another shiver run through her. Even though he'd been dead, she knew it was *him.* Could feel his very essence as she looked at his face, because he spoke to her soul.

Alexander...

She wiped away more tears. The sadness seemed to move out of her very being, as if all the memories were somehow just under the surface of her skin.

But wait. Alexander...

She stiffened. Lifted her head. Blinked. And then blinked again. The person from the dream in the 1700s clothes with the blood on his shirt—that was the same person that she'd seen in flip-flops and an un-tucked dress shirt.

God. She put a hand to her throat. It all made *sense* now. All those other dreams. Those visions. Those intense emotions when she'd first met him. Of course.

Nathan O'Neil. Nathan...Alexander...*was* Nathan. They were the same soul. Just different lifetimes.

Which meant only one thing. That she was...Edwina.

Chapter Nine

BUT EARLY THE next morning, back at Cross Keys Condos, Ruby and Nathan didn't find anything.

"Damn it." Nathan brought his hand down hard against the window ledge in his dad's study. "We've searched everywhere—"

Ruby pointed to a tiny carving of a heart on the ledge. "Do you think that means we should look there?"

Nathan traced a fingertip on the wooden carving. "All those centuries..." He shook his head. "Well, let's find out what's underneath."

They examined the window ledge. On the underside was a hidden hinge. Nathan crouched down and lifted up the ledge.

Ruby kneeled down beside him. "I think there's something in there," she said.

He reached for a folded piece of yellowed paper tucked into the small cavity created where the window met the wall. Nathan handed the page to her.

She cupped it in her palm. "Looks like it's from the mid-to-late 1700s."

"Really? Wow. How do you know all this stuff?" Ruby noticed he was lightly running his fingers along his jawline.

"Oh, uh, it has to do with the weight of the paper and the materials used." She frowned to cover the way her heart raced. "I should really go get my cotton preservation gloves." But she didn't move. She could feel the warmth of him as he crouched beside her in the tiny alcove created by the dormer window.

She unfolded the antique page. "Oh!" She scanned the flowing script. "It's a poem." She held it up.

Nathan's eyes widened and he gave a short laugh. "What? Is that the *original* version of *The Fair Isle Lovers*?" He shook his head slightly. "And it looks like it's even signed by Molly McDuff. Everyone on the island who knows their history, knows that Molly was the first barmaid at Cross Keys Tavern."

"So that was in addition to her being the first postmistress?"

Nathan nodded.

"You keep referring to that poem,"

Ruby said.

"Every school kid on the island had to memorize it. We'd all recite it during our grade six graduation ceremony. Island tradition." As he met and held her gaze, he began to speak from memory:

Though the sea 'twas bottle-green
A love like theirs has n'er been seen
Except on stormy, windy nights
When the moon is high & bright
You can still hear her true love call
The best and most handsome of them all
But when tragedy did befall
That fateful December night
'Tis said if one but wait for the light
Of the waning moon
Their hearts shall once more unite
Under glittering stars, black satin night
When the compass rose sheds its light
And all is, at last, set to rights

Ruby looked at Nathan with wide eyes. "This poem," a smile broke out on her face, "is *about* the compass. And if we find the compass, then we may find the seal, too."

"How do you know that?"

"The..." She blinked. "A dream," she

said softly. Slowly. "That I had last night...it was about—" her eyes darted everywhere but Nathan's face, "—two lovers who weren't meant to be kept apart. And it's a clue. I see it all so clearly now. And this poem, it's a clue trail that will lead to the whereabouts of the compass. Because that's what your dad was onto. The treasure he referred to that the British wanted, must have been the compass. And the legend... He knew they were connected. And that memory, it's in the poem. It's all in the poem. It's real, Nathan." Her eyes widened. "And it's up to us to find the compass so we can restore history as it was meant to be written. As Edwina and Alexander would have wanted it."

"Wait," Nathan said. "The poem isn't referring to the compass... But to the compass rose." He tapped his finger against his chin. "My painting... Edwina was holding a rose bud."

Ruby cocked her head. "So we're not looking for a literal compass rose... We're looking for a rose. A rosebush, I think. Maybe. Could that be why I've been smelling wild roses...?"

"Wait, you've been smelling wild roses too?"

Ruby nodded.

"And I don't think it's just any rose-bush," Nathan murmured. "I think it needs to be a rosebush with red-and-white blooms. Like the one in the painting I did."

"So you're saying if we look for a rose-bush, we'll find the compass?"

"Exactly," Nathan said. "And maybe even the seal, too. Hmmm. That rosebush... The poem mentions rose-red moonlight."

"One of Alexander's letters had a secret message that referred to rose-red moon-light, too," Ruby added.

Nathan nodded and glanced down at the page Ruby held. "That's strange. There are different ending lines. I mean, more of them..."

"Oh, you mean this?" She pointed to a stanza at the bottom:

The tale does not end
If you take the roses' path
To where it all began

"Another clue," Nathan said. "Sounds pretty literal."

Ruby nodded. "But where?" She glanced at the page again and pointed. "What's that?"

"Looks like a sketch of a canon."

"So that would mean some sort of military reference. Where were canons here in the 1700s?"

"Well, it wasn't the battery along the boardwalk. That was built in the1800s. So the only other place that would've been defended was Fort Amherst."

"Looks like that's where we're headed." Ruby got up.

"Come on," Nathan said, "Let's go."

RUBY GLANCED OVER at Nathan as he drove along the South Shore Route—Highway 19—toward the fort. "There's so much to think about."

"Maybe that's the problem." Nathan tousled his hair. "We're both thinking too hard."

Nathan's thoughts flicked back to the previous evening. What had happened there on the porch last night? All those thoughts swirled around in his head...

Thoughts that were memories. Memories of another time and place...memories of love and desire and heartache...as he'd watched Ruby. As he'd felt her fingers on his bare skin.

He took a deep breath and the racing thoughts faded.

Ruby had been affected too. His breath caught. He'd seen it as he'd looked into her eyes. How those same expressions had flitted, one after the other, across her face, too. Love. Desire. Heartache.

He and Ruby were...connected. Yes.

Nathan pressed his foot harder to the accelerator. The Lexus's engine screamed in protest as morning light crept across the rolling hills and pine forest.

He gripped the wheel. His stomach swooped as the car descended the hill and rounded the curve. The dusky green pine trees, brighter green potato fields and yellow-green of pastureland whipped by in a blur.

He barely glanced in the rear view mirror. He fumbled as he rolled down the driver's side window, but kept one eye on the road and one hand on the wheel.

He inhaled deeply. Felt his whole body relax: his attention sharper, clearer, as the fresh cool morning air entered his lungs. As a sense of exhilaration zipped through him.

Sunlight sparkled off the Northumberland Strait. Nathan adjusted his sunglasses.

As the red car wound along the gray ribbon of road, Nathan noticed Ruby clutched the seat cushion but she said nothing.

He eased his foot off the gas pedal and slowed the car. He topped a hill. The merest hint of a rutted red dirt track curved off to his right.

The light of dawn strengthened to golden morning as he turned the wheel and eased the car into the deeply rutted route just off of Highway 19. Dirt scraped the undercarriage as he inched along the familiar road.

Moments later, he turned off the engine and they both got out. The wind carried the scent of salt and the cry of seagulls.

Nathan looked out over the ridge as the sun began to glint off the calm waters of the strait. His eyes finally came to rest on the wrought iron fence that surrounded the small graveyard. Gnarled oaks and twisted paper birches guarded the entrance.

"This isn't Fort Amherst," Ruby said.

"No," Nathan said. "I just need to do something first. You'll be okay for a sec?"

Ruby nodded, and Nathan set off.

He walked down the grassy path and his attention turned to the gravestones in front of him. The dirt had settled some since he'd been here last, but the bouquet of carnations still leaned against one specific red granite headstone.

He sank to his knees in the soft earth and traced a fingertip along the carved words. "Hi Mom," he said in a low voice. "Well," he sighed and a half-smile tugged at his lips, "I'm in love. She's not even from here. And she's American, on top of that. But, well, her name's Ruby and she's so sweet. Beautiful." He gave a soft laugh. Shifted to a crouch. "I'm beginning to think I've known her, before." He shook his head. "Crazy, right? But I had to come out here and tell you. I know, I know. It's not logical or rational or any sort of left-brain thing. But I'm beginning to think that doesn't matter. That that's not how love works."

As NATHAN CONTINUED the drive over to Fort Amherst, Ruby sat in the passenger seat. Her fingers brushed the surface of the locket and her eyelids fluttered. Suddenly she was standing in a drawing room.

She saw green-and-white striped wallpaper. Heavy green velvet curtains with gold tassels at the windows.

And a man.

He stood with his back to her. She moved her gaze upward. Took in his tailcoat and the way the lightweight navy blue wool fell away to reveal long lean legs. The shiny brass buttons at the small of his back. The lace at his cuffs. The neatly tied cravat. And that glossy black hair tied in a queue at the nap of his neck.

Alexander.

He turned around, but his gaze slid right through hers. She was the ghost. Not him. She followed his gaze as the study door opened.

Ruby gasped. Because she was looking at herself.

She knew it the second she saw those green eyes. Green eyes that held the reflection of her own soul.

Ruby studied the cobalt blue silk dress, the pale skin, the blonde hair curled into neat ringlets. "Alexander," the woman whispered, a red-and-white rosebud in her hand.

"Edwina," he said. He took a step toward her, kissed the back of her hand. "Edwina," he repeated, and Ruby felt her toes curl at the loving caress of his voice, his tone. "Let me paint you."

She smiled up at him, stroked his cheek, then reached up and wound her arms around his neck. He put his arms around her waist. "Yes, Alexander," she whispered, just as their lips met. "For you, I will."

Ruby blinked and the images faded. She rubbed her arms to dispel the goose bumps. She turned to Nathan, her eyes wide, her lips parted.

He met her gaze. "So you saw them too," he whispered.

She saw his knuckles tighten on the wheel. He gave a shaky laugh. "So either we're both going crazy...or..." He glanced over at her.

Ruby licked her suddenly dry lips and nodded. "...Or I'm the reincarnation of Edwina."

"And I'm the reincarnation of Alexander."

Chapter Ten

THEY ARRIVED AT the national historic site. No cars were in the lot and all the lights were off in the interpretive center. And when they got out to look at the grounds, long yellow strips of caution tape criss-crossed the entrance. A couple of small bulldozers and a backhoe were parked along the perimeter beside a cement truck.

"Now what?" Ruby muttered under her breath.

"Looks like they're re-paving the side-walks and part of the lot." Nathan said. He turned off the engine and got out of the car. "We didn't come this far to stop now." He popped open his truck and pulled out a small folding shovel. "Never know when we might need this. Normally I keep it in here in case I get stuck in snow drifts in the winter."

"But..." Ruby said.

"I know the head maintenance guy. And the main desk guy. Besides, we're going, most likely, in the opposite direction of where they're working."

Ruby put her hands on her hips. "But we can't harm the historical or structural integrity of anything." She threw him a long, rather speculative look.

Nathan hoisted the shovel over his shoulder. "Of course not."

"Then all right."

Ruby had tucked the poem into a manila folder that she now had under her arm. She frowned. "Where did you say the rose bushes were?"

Nathan pointed toward the cliffs. "Over there. Through the pines. There's a whole row of them. Might as well start there."

Ruby followed him through a winding gravel path that led through towering pines, their dark green shapes somehow comforting to her.

Their shoes crunched under the gravel and Ruby could smell the salty air.

"So, the stanza's led us here," Nathan said, and came to stand by Ruby. She could smell his aftershave—a woodsy pine scent.

She glanced up at him. Nodded. "But we don't know where to go at this point. There aren't any other clues." She plucked the sheaf of paper out from the folder and held it in her hands. Dawn filtered through the antique yellowed page.

"Hey," Nathan said, and pointed at the blank space just below the last stanza. "What's that?"

Ruby twisted the chain of the locket around her fingers. "What's what?"

"There's more to this clue." Nathan's voice lifted. "Do you see that, right below the last stanza? It looks like...Here, can I take a look for a second?"

"Uh, sure." Ruby handed him the page.

He held it up to the morning light and angled the page so that she could now see what he meant. "It's another line of text," she said.

"Not just one," Nathan said. "Several..." He peered closer. "Whoever wrote it must have pressed the quill point hard enough that it left an indentation on the next sheet of paper. And then they used the sheet two or three sheets beneath the one originally written on, as the means to convey the message." Then he began to read.

Chained up hearts
To set them free
Use the lock
As the key

"Hmmm." Ruby frowned and fiddled with her locket. "Maybe it'd make more sense if we read the whole thing together. I mean the two stanzas that are clues."

The tale does not end
If you take the roses' path
To where it all began
Chained up hearts
To set them free
Use the lock
As the key

"So we've followed the roses' path," Ruby said, gesturing to the pale pink blossoms. They clung to the profusion of wild rose bushes that grew with abandon along the cliff's edge.

"But it ends here," Nathan said. He raked a hand through his hair and gestured to the rose bushes that petered out.

"What's beyond there?" Ruby asked as she pointed to the edge of the property.

"Just the woods. It's owned by Parks Canada but they haven't really done anything with it. There's some old foundations and stuff out there, apparently, but they haven't had the budget to develop them just yet."

"Foundations of what?"

"Houses, outbuildings, that sort of thing," Nathan said.

"We have to keep going."

"Look!" Nathan pointed to a faint red dirt footpath barely visible through the dense green undergrowth dotted with the occasional wild strawberry plant.

Purple asters poked through the foliage. Tall pines stretched to the sky as if they created a tunnel.

Nathan and Ruby walked along the faint trace of path for several minutes until Ruby spotted an area of the woods that looked as if it had once been cleared of its trees. New-growth forest poked its way through the dense underbrush.

Neither of them said anything as they both got closer.

Ruby met Nathan's gaze. "I was wrong," she whispered, and shook her head. "About so many things." She sighed. "But there's nothing here."

Nathan glanced around too. "Except for that." He pointed to the far corner of what looked like a huge mound of earth, but what, Ruby realized, as she stepped closer, was a pile of stones. But not just any pile of stones. A foundation. "A cabin," she breathed.

She followed Nathan as he approached the ruins. A gnarled, bent and crooked chestnut tree nearly five feet wide grew nearby. Its roots pushed the stones away from the remains of a rotting wooden doorframe.

"Look!" She pointed at the lintel. "There's that same heart carving as at Cross Keys! Just on the corner there. This has to be the right place."

"Nice work," Nathan smiled at Ruby. "And look here." He nodded at a rosebush, which grew near what was once the doorway, its last few red-and-white blooms nearly spent.

They knelt on the ground beside it. Nathan carefully began to spade over red dirt.

But as the sun continued to rise and the pink streaks of dawn gave way to bright daylight, each shovelful resulted in nothing.

After long minutes, she looked up at him. "I'm sorry."

"I know," he said. His voice caught over the breeze that gusted through the birch and oak trees that surrounded the small clearing. Ruby got up and went around the perimeter of the ruins, Nathan close behind.

As she made her way back to the chestnut tree, Ruby gasped. "I didn't see it from the other side of this tree, but look. Next to the rosebush? The chestnut tree's roots made what must have been the interior wall heave. I think there's something there."

Nathan crouched down beside her.

"I think if we just pull here..." She pressed her fingers into the small exposed crevice and tucked them under the tiny lip. As their fingers interlaced, and the stone shifted, he felt a jolt pass between them.

Nathan shone his light in the dark cavity. "It's some sort of handmade box." He reached in and picked it up. It weighed next to nothing. Intricate marquetry work in floral designs decorated the lid.

"Here. I don't want to spoil the surprise for you. You do it."

Ruby smiled up at him and took the box. It opened easily.

But there was nothing inside.

She scrubbed at the red dirt on her hands and under her nails then sat back on her heels and sighed. The morning sun filtered through the trees and she glanced at Nathan. "We've come all this way..."

Nathan met her gaze. "Not for nothing, Ruby. At least we've made it this far. The legend was real. The compass, well, at one point anyway, had been real. Before someone else solved the clues and found it. Or who knows, maybe even Molly decided to keep it herself. We just don't know. But at least we tried."

"Yeah, I guess you're right." She fiddled with the locket around her neck. She twined her fingers through the fine silver chain. Stroked a thumb along the heart-shaped surface. "Chained up hearts," she murmured to herself.

"That's referring to Edwina and Alex-ander. They were chained up. Well, probably not literally. But they were prisoners," Nathan said.

"Right," Ruby muttered as she looked down at the locket in her hands. She looked up at Nathan, her eyes wide. "What if...?" She reached up to unfasten the locket from around her neck.

As she cradled it in the palm of her hand, she said, "Chained up hearts. It's the *locket*. Something about the locket has to do with the seal. The compass. I mean, that's where the first clue was."

"True," Nathan said as he looked at the locket. "If you're right, then 'use the lock as the key' means...the locket itself is the key."

"Yes but we've already opened the box. There's nothing inside."

"Unless..." Nathan cocked his head. "It's one of those puzzle boxes? Sometimes they used special inlaid wood designs to disguise hidden compartments."

Ruby fumbled with the locket a second before she snapped it open. "But I don't see how—"

"Here," Nathan said, "on the inside of the box. Do you see that design?" He angled the box to catch the morning sun. "Yes... There?" He indicated a starburst shape on the underside of the box's lid. There's a tiny indentation where the sides and top of the box meet. It's the exact shape of—"

"This?" Ruby said, as she held up the locket. "There's a tiny groove in the back of the locket here. Don't know how I'd missed it before. Guess I just wasn't looking for it, so I didn't see it." She held Nathan's gaze a moment, paused, then put her fingernail into the groove. A small popping sound followed, and the whole back of the locket rose up. "I think you're supposed to twist this around..."

She put action to words and flipped the back around so that the pointed part of the heart now faced up, as if it was a key. "This must have been what that one diary entry of Edwina's meant. She had Revere craft the locket for her with this mechanism."

Ruby's fingers trembled slightly. Nathan placed his hand on top of hers. "Here," he said, "let's do this together."

With both of their hands on the locket-key, they fit it into the slot. There was an audible click. The top of the box popped open.

"Edwina must have concealed it in here after she realized she had to hide it when the governor discovered her in his private office." Ruby reached out and touched a fingertip to its shiny gold surface as it lay nestled among layers of rotted muslin.

"The compass of true love," Nathan said. He looked up and met her gaze. "We've found it at last."

"Yes," she breathed, as a smile spread across her face. "We have," she whispered, then gently picked it up. Nathan reached out and closed his fingers around hers.

"Their hearts shall once more unite
Under glittering stars, black satin night
When the compass rose sheds its light
And all is, at last, set to rights"

"God, Ruby." He reached up and

stroked a fingertip down her cheek, then cupped his fingers under her chin and tilted his head. *"...how my heart longs but for the taste of your kiss, the feel of your arms around me,"* he whispered, as a slow blush spread across Ruby's cheeks and her eyes widened.

"You knew?"

"Yes," he whispered, "I finally figured it out." He brought his other hand up to stroke the nape of her neck. She shivered as his fingers caressed her skin.

He trailed his hand back down her arm. Stroked his thumb across the back of her hand before he picked it up and pressed his lips to the thin skin there.

"I was so afraid of losing you," she whispered. "That's why I ran away all the time, from all those men. I wasn't afraid of commitment. They just weren't you, so I couldn't commit to them. That's why I left that afternoon. I'm sorry. It was Edwina's fears and worries I was carrying around into this lifetime. She was afraid of losing Alexander. She'd gotten there too late."

"And he had thought she'd abandoned him. Deserted him. Chose her own heritage, her own people, over him." Nathan held Ruby's gaze then withdrew his lips from her hand and interlaced their fingers together.

"I think part of me knew it all along but I was just resisting. I clung so long to logic and rationality that I forgot what it felt like to feel with my heart. I'd closed off that part of myself. But it wasn't really closing myself off, being emotionally unavailable to all those other women. I was simply waiting—to be with you, my love..." He skimmed his lips along her wrist and up her arm.

"Because with you, I already knew the truth. That you and I were meant to be together. That's why we came together in this lifetime. So we could finally realize that." He intertwined their fingers together and ran a thumb across her palm.

She reached up and placed a hand on his chest.

"Yes," she whispered, and leaned into him. She cupped the compass in her hands and looked up at Nathan.

He watched as the needle spun crazily for a moment and then came to rest, pointed directly at him. Then she handed the compass to him.

He held it up. Sunlight glinted off its polished face as the needle swung around and pointed in Ruby's direction.

Nathan brushed a strand of hair out of

her eyes. "Dad was right."

She smiled up at him. "I'm not going to say I told you so, because there were times when I doubted it too. But yes he was." She grinned, leaned in, wrapped her arms around his neck and pressed her cheek against his chest.

But the buzz of Nathan's cell phone in his pocket made her jump back.

Nathan dug out his phone. "Evie? What's up?"

"Nathan, you'll never believe it! When I was cleaning the twins' room this morning, I found a wrinkled, folded up piece of paper in their dollhouse. I thought it was just trash so I was about to throw it out but the feel and color of the page made me stop and unfold it. From what I understand from their disjointed story, Dad somehow had shown them the order. Guess he wanted to give them an appreciation for history. Anyway, one of the girls—they both tell me it was the other—kept it. They were playing post office with it all these months." Evie gave a incredulous laugh. "So Dad's name can now be cleared of the forgery charges."

Nathan let out a long, slow sigh and closed his eyes for a moment. "Thank God. We'll all go out to dinner tonight to celebrate."

Nathan ended the call and relayed the news to Ruby. "Now we can clear up this whole business with the UPEI Board of Governors and that committee, too."

"But we haven't found the seal."

"No, we haven't." He paused and cocked his head. "Hmmm. But I do know what happened to it now. Because in one of the dreams I had, I remember Alexander's brother took the seal from him when he was in Massachusetts. Said he was going to melt the seal down for coinage."

Ruby nodded. "That letter I found in Edwina's journal mentioned the same thing."

"The compass was really the treasure," Nathan added. "And the poem points to the compass, and the compass is clearly real, so now they'll *have* to validate Dad's research, even though the seal no longer exists. I'll talk to my lawyer tomorrow about this. She'll be able to get everything arranged. My dad," Nathan's arms tightened around Ruby's waist, "wasn't the crackpot everyone thought he was. Thanks to you."

She reached up and put a hand on Nathan's cheek. "I'm so glad. And thank you," she said softly, "for everything that *you* did for me. Because if it wasn't for you, I wouldn't have found out the truth."

Nathan grinned. "And you know what the first thing I'm going to do is, after talking with the governors and lawyer tomorrow?"

"What's that?" Ruby asked.

"Design a website for Edwina Belliveaux and Alexander McEachern. Edwina mentioned his last name in one of the journal entries. So everyone knows exactly what happened. They—we—deserve it."

"With what we've found," Ruby said, "I can finish my research now. And then I'll contribute that to your site." She paused. "I want to stay here on the island. That's why it felt so familiar when I stepped off the plane that first time. And why I couldn't stay away. Because it'd been home for me—and for Edwina—all those years ago. And now I'm free to stay here." She looked into Nathan's eyes. "I know why I've been yearning for a place to belong. I thought it was because I was adopted. And that was part of it. But it was also because of my past life as Edwina. She, as me, knew all along that P.E.I. was home. I just had to discover it, too."

"And Edwina and Alexander's story would've remained hidden from history...forever." Nathan reached up and brushed back a strand of hair that had blown into Ruby's eyes. "Until you came along. And until I realized that she and you were one and the same."

Ruby felt a thrill of happiness shoot up her spine. "You mean...?"

"I mean," Nathan said, as he smiled at her, "that now I'm convinced past lives do exist. They're as real as...well, you and me."

He leaned in, and she could smell his woodsy aftershave again. She tilted her head up, and threaded her fingers through his thick silky black hair.

"You know what else?" he whispered. "I'm going to paint a picture of Alexander and Edwina together." He pulled back a fraction to look at her. "But what about your job offer? And your doctorate?"

"Well, after everything we've uncovered, I'll have to make a few tweaks to the dissertation after I defend it early next month, but after that, I'll finally be able to graduate with my degree. I've also been talking to your sister at the Public Archives," Ruby said. "They want to hire me, after all I've done to contribute to the history of the island."

"Are you sure? It's not the big city, and it's not tenure-track."

"I know," she said. "That's what I thought I wanted. But I discovered what I needed is right here. A sense of belonging. Home... You."

"Yes," he murmured. He stroked her cheek and then closed the small space between them as he pressed his lips against hers.

And suddenly, everything felt right. All that they'd been through. As if no time or distance or longing or yearning had ever existed. Because in that moment, there by the cliff tops in the sparkling August sunshine, all that mattered was that they were together. Again.

"You know what?" Nathan said, after a few minutes. "Even though we didn't realize it at the time, the compass was still working its magic. Waiting for us to be reunited." He grinned, and leaned his forehead against Ruby's. "Because I've found you again. You've found me again. And," he murmured, "this time, it's forever."

Thanks for reading! Want more treasure hunting and romance?

If you enjoyed *This Time It's Forever*, then don't miss Maggie's story in
Now It's For Always.
It's the second title in the Prince Edward Island Love Letters & Legends trilogy.

Visit www.jessicaeissfeldt.com
to find out more!

FOR A LIMITED TIME
GET YOUR FREE SWEET ROMANCE HERE!

Get your free copy of the sweet romance *Beside A Moonlit Shore*. Normally, it's $2.99, but this GIFT is yours FREE when you sign up to hear from author Jessica Eissfeldt.

When you sign up, not only will you get this FREE GIFT, but you'll also receive sneak peaks of Jessica's upcoming stories, have the opportunity to win prizes, get exclusive subscriber-only content...and more!

After her sea captain husband dies, schoolteacher Anna Hampton wonders if she'll find the courage to love again...beside a moonlit shore.

Go here to get started:
www.jessicaeissfeldt.com/yourfreegift

FOR A LIMITED TIME

Acknowledgments

Karen Dale Harris—developmental editor, whose excellent insights and suggestions helped me shape this story into its final form

Shannon Page—copyeditor, who had a great eye for detail

Jane Dixon-Smith—graphic designer, who gave me a beautiful cover for the story

Sabrina Volman and J. Esmee McAskill—beta readers, who kindly read and encouraged this story from manuscript to publication

Dr. Graham Lea—academic consultant, who patiently and kindly read and provided feedback on all the academic-related content

Author's Note

I'd always loved the movie *National Treasure*, but wished it had a bit more romance in the plot. When I came across the intriguing historical tidbit about the Great Seal of P.E.I. being stolen in 1775 by American privateers, my imagination took off. I knew I had enough historical facts to create a piece of fiction that could intertwine three things I love: history, romance and treasure hunts. I hope you've enjoyed it!

There are a few places in this story where I tweaked the historical events and the historical timeline to suit the plot.

According to real historical events, the French left Fort Amherst in 1768, not in 1775, as I have had it occur in the story. Cross Keys Tavern was torn down in the early 1900s but the red brick building that was built in its place does house Cross Keys Condos.

And the seal, truly, has never been found...so you might want to keep your eyes open. Who knows what's in your attic!